W9-DBJ-221

How She Knows What She Knows About Yo-Yos

Sarabande Books
LOUISVILLE, KENTUCKY

How She Knows What She Knows About Yo-Yos

Stories by Mary Ann Taylor-Hall

FIRST EDITION

Managing Editor
Sarabande Books, Inc.
2234 Dundee Road, Suite 200
Louisville, KY 40205

LIBRARY OF CONGRESS CATALOGING-IN-PUBLICATION DATA

Taylor-Hall, Mary Ann.
How she knows what she knows about yo-yos : stories / Mary Ann Taylor-Hall.
p. cm.
ISBN 1-889330-36-1 (cloth : alk. paper). — ISBN 1-889330-37-X (pbk. : alk. paper)
1. United States—Social life and customs—20th century—Fiction.
I. Title.
PS3570.A983H69 2000
813'.54—dc21 99-19816
CIP

Cover photograph: *Untitled* by Judith McKernan. Photo courtesy of the artist.

Cover and text design by Charles Casey Martin.

Manufactured in the United States of America.
This book is printed on acid-free paper.

Sarabande Books is a nonprofit literary organization.

Grateful thanks to Anonymous, Emily Bingham and Stephen Reily, Georgia Delano (in honor of Peggy Morton), William and Gail Gorham, Dick and Nancy Graham, Nana Lampton, the New York Community Trust, and Mr. and Mrs. Owsley Brown for their generous support of Sarabande Books.

For Jim

Acknowledgments

These stories originally appeared in the following publications, sometimes in different form:

The Chattahoochee Review: "How She Knows What She Knows About Yo-Yos"

The Colorado Quarterly: "The World's Room"

The Kenyon Review: "Advanced Beginners"

The Paris Review: "Banana Boats"

Shenandoah: "Todo el Mundo"

I want to express my appreciation to the crew at Sarabande—Sarah Gorham, Jeff Skinner, Kirby Gann, Kristin Herbert, and Kristina McGrath—whose camaraderie, competence, and general high spirits have made this project a great pleasure for me; to Charles Martin for his splendid design; to Sally Arteseros for the clarity and sensitivity of her editing of the manuscript; and to Geri Thoma, for going the extra two thousand or so miles in my behalf.

My thanks to Diane Freund, Dick and Sue Richards, John Schwartz, Cia

White, and of course Jim Hall for their indispensable readings of these stories.

And to my friends in the every-third-Tuesday group, wherein a couple of these stories were hatched, for the urgent ongoing conversation in which I hope we'll all still be passionately engaged when we're ninety-two.

Contents

HOW SHE KNOWS WHAT SHE KNOWS ABOUT YO-YOS

Here comes Yo-Yo Man. He's doing walk the dog, he's doing rock the baby. His eyes are neon green—they flash, they send off silver sparkles as they spin and loop the loop, they play "If You Got the Money, Honey," fast and high. In front of the Court House, he lets his yo-yo take off rolling down the sidewalk at the end of its tether, pulling him along after it, till with a flick of his long flat wrist he snaps it up into the palm of his hand again. "Good dog!" cries Yo-Yo Man, flashing his white teeth all around. "I'd rather have me a yo-yo than a hound dog," he sings out. "You know why? 'Cause it comes on home." He sends his yo-yo three times round the world. "I'd ten times rather fool with a yo-yo than a woman." It smacks back into his palm. "You fellers out there know what happens when you try to wind a string around a woman, don't you. End up with a mess of snarls—she won't climb up and she won't shake on down either one.

"You'd be better off to put your money behind one of these round beauties in your choice of color, I got 'em all—plus a star-spangle special plays 'Say Can You See' going down and 'Dawn's Early Light' coming back up again. We got raspberry Lucite with bubbles inside, or black with electric sparkles, which goes for a little more, but it does good in the dark, get you wide awake or sing you to sleep, ever which way you want to go. Just make a loop and slip it on your finger, like you was marrying it. You could do worse, and probably have, a time or two, if you're like me. You can sling it off to the side of you like so. Or flip it down backhanded while you think over the world situation. Or you could have a pair of them for the price of a movie. Then you could send them two suckers down together like they was twins or roll one down while you're bringing the other on home, never be lonely again."

Undella stands in the middle of the crowd, wearing her pith helmet, on her way back home from the money machine, watching Yo-Yo Man shoot the moon with two separate yo-yos, like a gunslinger with a six-gun on each hip. Back they come to him, down he slings them, one then the other, whoop, whoop. There they stay put, spinning in place, till he's good and ready for them to jump back to him. She likes the glad way they go down, and the ready spring they have, coming back again. She can already feel that glow-in-the-dark gold one lying in her hand flashy, ready to roll, biding its time.

Undella thinks she might have yo-yos in the blood. Her daddy had many a tale of his yo-yo-throwing days, before he took up with hardware, dry goods, and Undella's mama. That's how *he* did worse. He got loose by going on to Glory, where he might have had some wild times again for half a dozen years or so, before Undella's mama got up there with him to lay down the law. Undella's sorry for her daddy, but glad for herself. She doesn't think of her mama as dead. Her load just shifted, leaving Undella freed up and out from under at last, down here in the land of Day-Glo yo-yos, at the age of twenty-one. She's lost out on her prime, but doesn't intend to lose out on anything else. She wants to see and do. It's not too late!

She's got the money, and she's got the time, too. She can buy her a yo-yo or two or three. She fishes her roll of five twenties, brand-new from the Jeanie Can Do machine, out of her pants pocket and steps right up to the front of the crowd, peeling off a bill—Can Do!—to get the first sale in this town behind them. "I'll take your gold and your two-tone green," she says right out loud.

"You won't be sorry, I promise you, sister," he cries out, giving her his white-tooth smile of delight, while all around her the closed-tight faces are saying, *Uh huh, uh huh, her mama's money. She'll not have it long.* "You're making a good investment, you're not throwing your money away," he assures her, as if *he* knows what this crowd is thinking, too.

"And I don't intend to, either," says Undella, holding up her chin, pocketing her smooth new yo-yos, counting the change he gives her in flimsy been-around ones out of his cigar box. "Now all I need is yo-yo throwing lessons," she says, looking him straight in his spinny eyes, which, way back at the holding-still center, right while she's looking, get a bright idea. Get it, give it to her so fast *her* eyes get to spinning, too. Right there, for two or three seconds, it's like she's a helicopter, lifting off.

He gives her a happy smile. "It's a sin to need what you can get so easy," he says, winking at the crowd so fast she's not sure he did it. "You're looking at your lessons, sister."

She wants to see and do, but she's got a good head on her shoulders and knows when to use it. She's not the type to fall for a line and a look from some fly-by-nighter with a lot of teeth, especially a fellow that gives a wink he thinks she's too slow to see. He doesn't know she's every bit as sharp as *he* is, just not so showy. "How much will they put me back?" asks Undella, standing square under her sun helmet. She feels a lot of flat eyes on her, no spin in them whatsoever. She hears her mama's name murmured somewhere in back of her, *Mrs. Cantrell Jones. Spinning in her grave. That girl. Screw loose.* "Now, that depends on how far you want to go," he says, settling his shoulders to get serious. "I believe you're a born athlete, just to look at you—I'm satisfied I could have you spinning doubles and cat's cradles by this time tomorrow."

Undella's heart jumps at the idea of it, but she holds onto business, like somebody in a high-water river holding onto a low-hanging branch. "I'm not signing up till I hear what you go for per hour."

He throws down backhand, calculating, then looks back up at her, all business himself in the way he squints his eyes. "This particular night, I go for a real nice chicken dinner."

There is a general gasp from the crowd. She looks at him steady and says, "Then you've come to the right place," with all the mean eyes in the crowd sliding sideways—there's Lanta Pollard, who once was a majorette and can't forget it, giving Donnie Burgess a secret tight smile of knowing all about it, somebody behind her snorting a laugh through his nose, a sound Undella hates—why can't they open their mouths and laugh like they were tickled instead of just confirmed in their suspicions? Mr. Danzell from the drugstore with his blue almost-crossed eyes stares outraged down his long narrow nose.

Yo-Yo Man nods at her, a substitute handshake, *done deal,* then jerks his head up, leaps onto the bench dedicated to the Korean War, and gathers that crowd's attention back to him by whooshing his yo-yo out in a semicircle around him, like clearing a swath with a scythe, catching it backhanded, twisty wristy, on the other side of him. "Now then, who all else is going to be happy before the sun goes down?"

Undella stands back now—she was already happy at ten o'clock in the morning, that's what he doesn't yet know about her, along with much else. For instance, Undella can do things with a chicken this boy never heard of. He's thinking KFC but she's thinking *Joy of Cooking*. She bought that cookbook for a dime out of the library sale. She wants to educate herself, make up for the years she watched her mama cooking the beans olive green and the pork chops gray and plain, or covered in white gravy. She always knew there must be more to life than that.

More to life than Bible Study class every Sunday morning. Than that patch of lawn, with marigolds and begonias scrunched up along the edge, more to life than the plaid old-lady dresses her mama sewed for her all through high school, when the other girls had on their tight peekaboo jeans.

She needs to get back to the situation she walked off from, but she can't tear herself away from him pulling dollars out of this tightfisted crowd, giving yo-yos in return. It's an education, just to watch the way he sizes up someone and guesses what kind of yo-yo they can't live without and then he gets down into his sack and finds it, throws it right to them and winds it on back, like he was casting live bait to a big old smallmouth bass, setting his heels and his jaw to reel them on in.

Besides, they haven't agreed on the time and the place.

While she's watching him, one trick tumbling out after another, she tries her best to imagine a life for such a one. Where does he put that burlap sack down in the evening, for instance? What would it take for him to go to sleep a happy man? Not much—he looks like he's happy all day long and far into the night, just like her. She doubts an unhappy man could do those round the worlds—she can tell they call for a loose and joyful spirit. She looks him over—he's a long drink of water in his low-slung blue jeans and satiny black cowboy shirt with mother-of-pearl in the studs, but those boots are walkers not riders, from the dusty scuffs of them. He's got a white straw cowboy hat tipped back on his head and yellow flowers around his neck like those leis the hula girls of Hawaii wear, only his are plastic. She wonders where he's from—not Oxford County, Kentucky, is all she knows. If anything as out of the ordinary as Yo-Yo Man came from within thirty miles of here, she'd surely have heard.

She would like to find out exactly what type of bed a fellow like that would need to make him sleep sound. He has tall bones and restless sharp moves that probably give out fast and without much notice underneath him. He looks flashy and temporary. What kind of mattress would settle him down? He's got an edgy manner, like he's been sleeping rough and not enough. But some fellows, she guesses, easy living might make them lose their snappy edge.

What Undella left off from when she decided to take a break and walk the four blocks up from her house to the bank—and it shows in her shirttail hanging out and her dirty-kneed work pants—was stone-wall building, which is the most opposite you could get from yo-yo throwing, because in stone-wall building, what you *put* down *stays* down, makes something out of itself besides just thin air and fancy memories. Now, that tall skinny number looks like he's ready to climb his own string up to heaven selling yo-yos to the angels all the way, and that's fine, that's pretty, but what good would pretty do her, and a string of plastic flowers, if it couldn't heave a stone to her when she got up over her head on that wall she's building between her and the parking lot of the Macedonia Baptist Church? She wants it high as a Baptist's eyes. That's all the higher it needs to be. But now she's made an investment in yo-yos, and she owes it to herself to follow up on this other side of life where things rise up pretty much on their own, just because you want them to, with no effort on your part except a come-here with your finger.

When there's finally not a soul left to sell to, he gets back around to her, making a toy revolver out of his forefinger and thumb and pointing at her, clicking. "Now then, pretty lady," he calls out, "what about this lesson you was wanting?" Pretty lady, my foot, she thinks, but when he calls her that, joy rolls up Undella in a big slow wave. He hoists up his sack and crosses the grass toward where she's waiting, in the shade. "Name your where and your when," he says, "and I'll be there. People call me Slip, what do they call you?"

"They call me Stony," she says, right back at him, because two can play that game. "Whenever suits you, after four."

"I still got to go work the Big Lots. Let's say five, seeing how hard these folks around here hang on to their cash money. And if you want two lessons, Stony, you better book now. Because once I'm gone from here you won't see me again for a while." He says it like he's warning her to get used to it.

"What'll the second one cost?"

He tips his hat at Undella. "Same as the first, if you pass the test."

He must be as hungry as he looks. "You talking breakfast now?"

"Whatever you want to call it. Something to hold me till I make Mt. Sterling."

"I'll fix you something to hold you till you pretty near make West Virginia, if you get me spinning yo-yos. I'll meet you at five in the parking lot of the Baptist Church back yonder in there," she tells him, waving her hand.

He gives her a look with his lit-up eyes and teasy grin. "Sounds holy," he says.

Undella looks right back. "*Could* be holy."

○

Before she starts in building her stone wall again, Undella walks along Pike Street to the PicPac. She has decided on the recipe named Chicken

Ferocious, because she's made that one before and thinks it might get his attention. She can do it in the backyard, throw some corn in a pot. Now she is leaning over the meat case, picking out their best cut-up chicken. The mirror over the meat shows her a fine, sturdy girl, with brown eyes deep and steady. Her hair is packed up under her pith helmet, but some of it straggles down around her cheeks. She turns her head to the side—she knows those butchers behind the mirror are watching, so she does it fast—to get a glimpse of her lips that curl upward at the corners even when she's not smiling, like a cat's, and her turned-up pink nose and pointed chin. She thinks she's a nice four-wheel-drive type of girl, strong for her small size and reliable, sucking on a peppermint. She never heard *pretty* before, but she knows she's too good to waste and plenty good-enough-looking to be walking around in the world, except for a smudge of dirt on her face and her dirty old work shirt. In produce, she picks up a head of cabbage for her secret-ingredient coleslaw. Tiny peas from the freezer. Some Valencia oranges, three for a dollar. A Hershey bar, with almonds—she can't resist, although she already has a nice plum cobbler for dessert that she made up last night from Baptist plums that fell on her side of the fence. She'll worry about Meal Number Two when and if.

She carries the groceries home, chops onions, sets her barbecue sauce to simmering, shreds her cabbage and puts it in ice water, and then goes out to start on the wall again.

In the twelve-foot opening between her garage at the back and the tall hedge fence of Mr. and Mrs. Foosie next door, her backyard is like a stage where the Baptists could hold an outdoor drama, if they set up chairs in their parking lot. Just turn on the porch light here. Undella's mama took pride in passing the Baptist muster. She was one *of* them. All she had to do was walk across the alley and there she'd be, with people who were up to her. When they called to her to bring some of her nice zinnias for the altar, she'd run to get her scissors.

The Baptist Church wanted to step right in and take the place of Undella's mama for her, but Undella sent those Circle ladies hurrying to find themselves some other orphan. She never minded the hymn singing, just the fast eyes on her business.

She has her own ideas about Sunday mornings, as she does about a lot of things she's never gotten to try out—for instance, she'd like to get out of bed at dawn and swing in her hammock and watch the light come up without worrying about being seen. That's why she needs a wall.

Or what if, one fine day when it comes time for Sunday school, some hot car well-known around this town should turn up parked in her driveway, left over from Saturday night? It never has happened yet, not once, but if it *did*. She thinks lack of a privacy fence has been keeping her whole love life away. What kind of a fellow would volunteer to be checked out by the Committee on Who's Where When. "Company, Undella?" they'd ask sweetly, their eyes running off to see if anyone they knew might be hiding behind the yew hedge. Once she's got her a privacy wall, who knows what might happen? Undella can hardly wait to find out.

It's getting on to three feet high now. She wants it seven at least. She's done a good job, so far—the wall's thick and solid, not a wobble in it, the rocks slapped flat together in even rows. It calms her down just to look at it.

She's about used up her latest load of rock. She'll have to take her truck out to her Uncle Nestor's farm and pick up some more from out of his sorry fields. "Here comes Rocky Three, haw haw haw," her uncle always yells. "What's she need all them rocks for? You reckon she's fixing to find her a man and build a fence around him?" She hates to go out there. But it's her only supply source.

At four o'clock, she comes in from her wall building and runs a bath. She washes her hair and, on an upsplash, comes out of the water with an inspiration. She wraps a towel around her and goes to her mama's bedroom and kneels down to open the bottom dresser drawer, where, underneath her mama's flannel nightgowns, which she hasn't gotten around to packing up yet, wrapped in tissue paper and never once worn or even tried on, as far as Undella knows, lie the silk pajamas that Uncle Chuck sent back for Undella's mama from Vietnam, long ago, before Undella was even born. In the uproar and confusion of the fighting, he must have temporarily forgot who his sister was—or maybe she was different when she was in her own young days. Undella's lucky her mama didn't cut them up and make sofa cushions out of them. Gold, heavy, with a soft silky shine, and a beautiful green dragon on the back, to match Undella's choice of yo-yos, right down to the two tones of green.

She puts on the top—the bottoms are way too long and won't stay rolled up, so she settles for her jeans, then stands in front of the mirror, blow-drying the home permanent she gave herself for her mama's funeral. That was harder than building the wall, winding up all those tiny rollers with no help, but she had a good result. It told the whole town that she'd started a new part of her life. Her hair is her crowning glory, that's what her daddy told her once, the color of dark cherry wood. And now it's curly, too, halfway down her back, so that she looks to herself like a high-spirited pony, roan-colored, wild-eyed. She tousles her hair with her fingers while she's drying it, to get it way out there.

When she's got herself ready, she slips on her flip-flops and goes down the steps into the backyard, hikes herself onto the wall, and swings her legs over it. She practices for a while on her own with her green yo-yo. She's saving the gold one for good. All she can do so far is throw it down and yank it back up into her palm.

After the heaviness of rocks, the yo-yo feels like a bubble, a little round hope on a string. She's in the silky mood to sling that baby way on out there, her gold sleeves sliding up and down her arms. But she's got a dragon on her back, she reminds herself, and twenty self-covered buttons going across the front, on the diagonal.

Slip rounds the corner, walking jaunty, with his burlap sack on his back, just as the Baptist bells strike five. When he sees her, he takes a step backward, holds up his free hand, and says, "Whoa." He comes closer, then brings his chin in and makes his eyes go wide, pretending he's knocked off his pins, but he's also showing that a girl would have to go a lot further to get him really off balance. "The young lady I was looking for wasn't wearing no goddess outfit. When last seen she was more the ready-for-action type."

"I'm ready for action," speaks up Undella, tossing her hair, then blushes at the bold, laughing way he takes her words.

But then he sets down his burlap sack by the wall and catches hold of the front brim of his hat and brings it down a notch, to show it's time to get serious. "Well then, let's begin, Stony. Because there's worlds to learn and every bit of it begins in the wrist." He lays a thumb on the underneath of her hand and a slim brown finger over the top of it, so as to snap her wrist up and down, up and down, then turns it over and bends it backward. "This is the secret of all yo-yo motion," he explains, his long face serious, "L-O-V-E" written across his four finger bones. Where his black shirt cuff is turned back, she can see the beginning of a tattoo on the inside of his arm—a fishtail, so it's doubtless one of those naked women at the top.

"No yanking. No elbow." He shows her what she's doing wrong

to make the green yo-yo go dead in its spin, to have the string tangle halfway back up. "But it ain't all you. You got to work the new out of a yo-yo. Give it here a minute. You got to limber up the string, get it to where it can feel exactly what you want it to do."

He unloops the string from her finger and rewinds it fast, paying attention. He's not afraid of tangles. They go with learning a yo-yo up one side and down the other. He takes this green one through its paces, one move sliding into the next so fast and smooth that Undella's out of breath by the time he gives it back to her. "*Now* try it, and pay attention," he says. When she messes up again and says, "Oh shoot," he says, "Just wind it up and start again. Be like the basketball players—you play, you foul. No apologies. No loser's attitude around here."

She wants to say, "That's one thing we don't have to worry about." But she's got to concentrate—it's going up and down pretty smooth now, just a slight wobble in the string from time to time. He sings out, "Good! That's good right there. It's getting worked out nice now. It's beginning to feel like it's really yours, ain't it!"

Undella nods, never taking her eyes off the green bobbing yo-yo fixed to her middle finger, rising and falling, rising and falling.

"Like you *oiled* it, right? And *now*—" He doesn't stop for breathers, he gives her her full hour's worth, he works for his chicken dinner, and Undella is picking up some moves. By the time the bells chime six, he's gotten her through basic throw-down, sling-forward overhand and underhand, shoot the moon, rock the baby, cat's cradle, and hesitation waltz.

On the way, he praises her to the skies. He tells her he never knew anyone to pick it up so fast. He tells her straight, like he really means it, that he believes she's a natural for the sport. They've got the basics out of the way, so the next lesson is open for finer points and showstoppers. This Slip is a born teacher, she can tell, a coach that drives you to the limit for one reason only, the love of yo-yos. Now they're onto round the world, and he throws in an extra five minutes. Undella's yo-yo goes around like she's launching a catapult, but it's way out at the end of its string and won't come back. She lets it die down and then drags it in, hand over hand, and begins rewinding it.

"You have to give it a little hitch, like it was a horse, and you're telling it, 'Come back home now, sweetheart.' You have to feel up your whole arm when it's right to bring it on in. There's a rhythm to it only you can tell. Take one loop, for now, and then bring it back." Undella nods, nestling the yo-yo in her palm like a pitcher getting ready to throw a spitball. "Round the world is where you learn if you're a real yo-yo outfit, or just some weekend up-and-downer. Round the world you got to use your shoulder and your hip, you got to go with the motion, feel it all up from the foot, till that string is just more of your leg and your side and your arm. You've got to move with it nice and easy, else you'll never get it home. People say oh, that's nice, that's cute, but good yo-yo throwing is like anything else—you got to go through difficult on the way to easy. You got to put in your time."

And now Undella's got round the world, too! She does it again, and then once more to show it wasn't any accident and smacks it back into her palm. "Oh, man!" says Slip, holding his hat brim and spinning around on the heel of his boot. "If I had you for a week or two, I'd make a champ out of you. You could go to yo-yo Olympics. You've got talent and drive, Stony, the most I ever saw, outside of myself. I mean that sincerely. One more time through everything I taught you, and then I'd say it's time to get after that chicken."

Oh, how Undella wishes Slip could have her for a week or two and make a champ out of her!

She's in need of a walk of life and this could be it, it could be!

Instead of going back to correspondence college to finish where she left off on bookkeeping when her mama took sick, a whole new idea is coming up in her heart. She's got to think of something fast, she knows that. What her mama and daddy saved in nickels and dimes isn't going to last forever—it looked like a treasure trove when she first came into it, but she's been drawing down on it. The first thing she did was to get her Uncle Chuck to teach her how to drive—twenty-one and can't drive is a crying shame on somebody. "No, *ma'am*," her mother would say when she asked, like she was putting her foot down to foolish ideas. Undella spent her first twenty years riding shotgun to her mama's thirty-five mph. As soon as she got her license, she traded in the hateful old Impala on a nice secondhand Chevy truck. The day she drove it home was the day she got the idea of the wall between her and the Baptists, so she needed a few other necessities, like an iron digger and a maul, plus groceries over the three months she's been living in the house by herself. That savings account is getting down now to numbers she can understand. It didn't take any time at all.

She wants to take care of herself. She wants to amount to something. Her plan has been to finish out the wall and go out and get a job she can hold while she gets through the last of her correspondence studies. But what if she could have a career in yo-yos! What if she could go here and there in her truck, selling yo-yos and seeing the world! She'd better be careful and not let this boy put ideas in her head. Except it's not his idea, it's hers. But he put it there, and it's doing shoot the moons around the thought of keeping books for E-Z Terms Used Cars on Bridge Street, where she got her truck, or working late shift at the DQ. In spite of herself, she's thinking about yo-yos and yo-yo T-shirts. A line of merchandise: hula hoops, croquet sets. She doesn't know what all.

After the lesson, the two of them climb back over the wall and thread their way through the loose rocks strewn here and there on the grass. "You know who's building this wall, don't you," she asks him.

"I reckon they don't call you Stony for nothing."

She nods, looking sideways at him.

"You're some kind of mighty one."

"That's right." She holds her arms up and curls her fists, flexing her muscles. "That's why I got a dragon on my back." She turns around to show him. He has to take and gather her hair to one side to see. The feel of his thumb sliding along the back of her neck gives her a slithery feeling.

"Hot zing! Breathing out a spray of fire, red, blue, and orange!" He lets go of her hair and smiles down at her real close and friendly. "I guess that's what they're talking about when they say holy smoke." Then he says, in a no-nonsense man-to-man kind of voice. "Where you getting your rock?"

"My Uncle Nestor's farm—he lives over toward Oddville."

He nods for a while, like he's trying to frame a question. "That's a nice kind of uncle, bringing you a load of rock whenever you need some."

"Oh, can't you just see old Nestor bringing me a load of rock!" she says merrily. "No. I go out and get it myself. Bust 'em down in the field, throw 'em up in my truck."

"Oh. *Now* I get it," he says. "You're one of those pickup-truck girls I've heard about."

"I guess," she agrees, cautiously, wondering what he's heard about them, but not wanting to ask. "And this is where I live," she tells him, and adds, to her surprise, "for now." Up until she said it, she would have sworn she'd say, "Always have and always will." But the whole deal is getting slidy now. Nothing says she has to live across the alley from the Baptist Church the whole rest of her life. No telling what she might do. She was thinking she needed a wall, but maybe all she needs is a plan.

She sits him down in her lounge chair and lights the charcoal in the barbecue grill. He leans back with his hands behind his head. "It's going to take another half-hour or so. Time you finish eating, you'll be going down the long road home in the dark, I expect."

"Don't worry about it, Stony—the dark is the same as the light to me. But I never said it was the road home. I'm into my summer tour, with many a stop before me. I'll show up tomorrow morning to give you Lesson Two, and then I'll be on my way."

Undella has to press her lips together to keep from wincing at the sound of those words! But she's not one to beg—she'll get Lesson Two and then just teach herself. Check out a library book. He doesn't hold the only key to yo-yos. "If I want Lesson Number Three, I'll have to give it to myself, I guess." She tries to say it in a jolly way, but it comes out pretty sad.

"Well, let's see how it goes," he says, light and cool.

In spite of herself, this causes an explosion of hope in her that makes her run inside and bring him out a pink lemonade and beer nuts for an appetizer. "Here you go, to tide you over." She has another idea and goes back and cuts some cheese into cubes and sticks toothpicks in every one of them, like when they have free samples on a tray at the PicPac, but when she comes back out, Slip's sound asleep in the lawn chair. Maybe he traveled the road to *here* in the dark.

She'll have to watch the chicken herself. Just as well. He'd let it burn, thinking about Mt. Sterling or wherever's next. And besides, the deal was she'd cook for him, and, to be fair, he's already done his side of the bargain. She wants to make hers extra good, so he won't forget where she lives. She doesn't look at him too close, out of politeness, but she can see his head is dropped to one side. He breathes deep, regular breaths, with no snores.

She runs back and forth to baste the chicken with the barbecue sauce, slice the German tomatoes, husk the corn, put her yeast rolls in the oven, set the picnic table under the sugar tree. Finally, he stirs behind her, turns, and gets his knees kind of tucked up, and she can't help noticing he's got right smart holes in his soles, blocked up with cardboard to keep the road out. He opens his eyes and smiles at her, a big, slow, half-asleep smile, like he's so delighted to wake up and find himself just where he always wanted to be. It turns her right around to give the chicken pieces another quick baste. "That smells like chicken to *me*," he allows, sitting up now, yawning and grinning and tipping back his hat to scratch his head.

"In case you wanted to wash up," she says, like her mama did when the Circle was at her house, "the bathroom's down on the left-hand side. There's towels out."

"You mean you're gonna let me in your house?" he says, teasingly.

It hadn't crossed her mind not to let him in her house. She thinks for a minute, then decides, *oh, well.* She's sharp enough to know a serial killer if she saw one. "Times when you've got to just hope for the best," Undella says.

"That's what *I* do. Nothing ventured nothing gained, the way I look at it."

"Anyway," she can't help adding on, "it would take two of you before I'd be scared, Slip, to be honest. You're tall but you're slight."

"Ain't you something." He studies her with his eyes half-closed under his cowboy hat.

"I got a dragon on my back, don't forget."

"There you go! Don't mess with the fire-breather!" He lifts

himself out of the chair now, unfolding himself like a jackknife with a lot of blades. She leads the way into the kitchen and sends him on down the hall, where she's laid out a blue towel and washcloth that match the fish in the shower curtain. She puts in the corn, then races back outside again.

After a while, he comes out the back door with his hat off, his brown hair slicked back with water. He's washed his face, too. He looks a little orphanish now himself, she sees, when she glances at him. Beat up around the edges of his face, but young in the middle, where his close-set eyes meet the bridge of his nose. Young and scrawny. He needs some joy of cooking, for sure. "Why don't you come and get the chicken off the grill for me?"

She goes back to the kitchen and brings out the rest of the meal on a tray. Slip claps his cowboy hat back on his head. "Stony, this could be in the magazines."

"Well, it's to eat, not look at—go on and help yourself," she says, pleased, sitting down facing the parking lot and her rock wall. She's beginning to see what it will look like when it's finished. Tall.

He loads his plate and eats steady and delicate and quick, while she sips her iced tea and watches, bashful about eating with company. "Now this is a meal *worth* an hour of work," he remarks.

That brings her to pick up her corn and get it buttered and salted and raised up to her mouth. "How'd you get the name of Slip?" she asks, wanting to get to the bottom of him. "From slipping out or slipping around?"

He gives her a bright look, like he appreciates her sense of humor, finishes his chews and then swallows, has a sip of tea, thinking it over. "It's just that I travel light. Light and fast. It used to be—in my early days—the next time you blinked I'd be in Richmond, Indiana, or Cairo, Illinois."

"I'm not blinking, then, until I get Lesson Two."

He looks at her like she was a book with pictures, taking his time, turning the pages, his head over to one side. "You sure are rarin' to learn yo-yos," he says at last.

"I know."

"Why's that?"

"I'm thinking of my future."

He nods deeply, then says, in a heartfelt way, "I sure wouldn't want no future that didn't have yo-yos in it."

She meant her financial future, but she wouldn't like him to know that now. They both eat their corn for a while—he goes wherever his mouth lands, she goes straight down and back.

"Where do you get your yo-yos, Slip?" she asks. His business is a puzzle to her.

"When I run low on merchandise, I get out my map and plan out where I mean to be in two days, and then I call my 1-800 and they ship out a batch to that place, C.O.D., in care of Hold for Pickup."

"How in the world do you get to all these places you go?" she asks. "You got no wheels, do you?"

"Nope. I got no wheels." He gives his head a sad shake. Then he pats his napkin to his mouth. "One of these days. Keep it simple and in the clear is my motto. Meanwhile, if I got some definite place I've got to make—a festival or flea market or county fair—I'll thumb a ride or go Greyhound. Otherwise, I walk—not the four-lanes, though. The back roads. I like to see the sights, I truly do. I enjoy my travels except for the dogs, but I carry a whistle that hurts them so bad they drop down and put their paws over their ears and cry.

"A lot of my sales opportunities are ones you don't know about till you trip over them—say a crossroads grocery with a half-dozen farmers on a rainy day, already wore out on whittling and card playing. Or maybe it's a laundrymat—people with nothing to do but look at three-year-old magazines—or a roadhouse with a few sad split-shift drinkers ready for something to light up their life."

Undella is listening hard, to get a handle on the day-to-day operations of Yo-Yo Man.

She's looking hard, too, trying to hold two things in her mind at the same time, the razzle-dazzler on the Court House square and the skinny man with holes in his boots walking some country road in the rain with a burlap sack over his back.

She shakes her head, to get rid of that idea. He wouldn't like to be felt sorry for.

"Not to brag, but I'm their best salesman. They say I could make a small fortune if I could cover more territory." Undella can't help sliding her eyes sideways toward her garage, where her new five-year-old short-bed Chevrolet truck is stashed away like money in the bank. "But I do pretty good, anyway," he goes on, seeming glad to share his life story. "If I don't sell a yo-yo, it won't ever be because I only gave it half a try!" He's taking quick bites of his chicken. He's about the nervousest eater she's ever seen. "Stony, this chicken's got a nice kick to it," he says.

And now, beyond her stone wall, a big buy-American Baptist car pulls into the lot, another one right behind it. "Oh shoot, shoot, shoot, it's those Midweeks," Undella says, putting her corn down on her plate and glaring across the fence. "I forgot this was Wednesday night."

Slip says, not understanding the emergency, "What's in this slaw that makes it taste so different?"

"Fresca," Undella blurts out, so rattled she gives away her secret ingredient without thinking.

"Well, no wonder, then."

Even though Undella's wall is three feet high now, Mrs. Clevis

Custer, thrashing up out of her Oldsmobile in her blue and white cotton with white matching earrings and necklace, catches sight of her right away. "Hello there, Undella!" she calls, with her big red smile and black eyebrows. "You having you a late supper, aren't you. What in the world you building there, darlin'? That looks like a sure-enough *something.* Oh, I'm sorry, honey, I just now noticed you had company."

Slip looks up at Undella over his chicken leg and rolls his eyes and licks his fingers, then turns sideways to tip his hat toward Mrs. Custer, and Mrs. Custer takes him in with her bright black eyes and nose built large for sniffing out trouble, and Undella can tell she's going to waddle right in on her white high heels to the Morals Committee to report on that lei of flowers that Slip still has around his neck.

"*Undella!*" he says now, grinning up to the gums. "Un*dell*a. Now that's a plentiful name. How come you told me Stony?"

"How come you told me Slip?"

"Because that's who I'm truly known as. That's what everybody calls me, Florida to Michigan, Slip Finnigan. Out-Again-In-Again Finnigan, that's me. I've close to forgot my real name, let's see, it's coming back to me—Thomas Alva Finnigan. Undella what?"

"Jones," she says crossly. "I hate those Baptists," she bursts out then. "I just can't wait to get my wall up."

"So everybody in town won't know you're feeding up the fast-talking low-living Yo-Yo Man?"

"Seems like they've only got my backyard to keep them interested in life."

"Why don't you just go inside and pull down the shades? The other thing is, of course, you could tell 'em to take a flying leap."

Undella laughs, shocked and thrilled. "Take a flying leap," she imagines herself saying to Reverend Griner and Mrs. Custer, and then sees them doing it, leaping, falling, flapping their arms, their plump legs running through high thin air.

"I reckon you should have gone to Lee's Famous, shoved a bucket of hot wings at me, and sent me on my way. Now look at the fix you're in." He gives her that teasing grin and takes a drink of iced tea, then gets a thoughtful distant expression on his face and comments, "They get a good turnout, don't they."

"Ha! Good luck—Saint Paul himself couldn't sell a yo-yo to one of those Macedonians." It gives her a charge to think of Old Preachy Paul from the stained-glass window with a yo-yo in his hand. "They'd think it was gambling or defiling the temple or something." Still, she knows there's a chance Slip Finnigan will just so happen to be under the arc light doing walk the dogs when the service lets out.

Now there's a dozen or so cars in the lot, a few stragglers turning in. Someone else is waving at Undella. Her Uncle Chuck, the one who gave her mother the pajamas she's got on the top of, twenty-five years ago. Maybe it's long enough ago that he won't remember. He's looking across at her, while handing his wife Clarissa out of the car. Clarissa is a slight, tight, brown-headed lady in way-high heels who sells lingerie part-time at Lazarus in Lexington and calls it her profession. Clarissa doesn't hold Undella in high esteem, and Undella thinks it's because Clarissa has been trained to see right through to her white cotton underpants. Uncle Chuck yells over at her, "You having a picnic, baby?" Slip glances over his shoulder again and gives a friendly nod, then turns back to look at Undella, interested.

"Something like that," Undella answers, taking a stone-faced bite out of her corn.

"Maybe Clarissa and me will come over after service and have a piece of chocolate cake with you and your friend."

Undella believes she can trust Clarissa to yank the chain on that idea, but just to be on the safe side, she swallows and says, "I'll let you know next time I do my double devil's food—maybe next Wednesday night, Uncle Chuck." Slip watches her, squinting one eye, thinking her over. When Chuck and Clarissa walk on into the sanctuary, Slip keeps looking at her, so she says, "What about seconds? Help yourself." And he does. He's storing up. He's getting while the getting's good. He can sure put it away, for a narrow man.

By the time he's about finished up, the Baptists are singing in a happy jigging way about how they were very deeply stained within. Slip, turning his third ear of corn into the butter on his plate, laughs and says, "You could dance to that."

"Ha!"

"You sure could." He puts down his corn and spins around on his bottom and gets up to show her, doing a slow silly knee-bending high-stepping elephant-type dance to show himself sinking deep in sin and then, when Mrs. Wilson the organist does a cute five-note run-up to the bouncy chorus, he spins his arms out in delight and goes a little bit wild, showing off the holey bottoms of his boots. "Love lifted me, *kick*, love lifted me." When the hymn is over, he claps toward the church, and Undella claps, too, flushed up as if she'd been dancing herself.

"How about if I turn on your radio to some Young Country, and then we could dance sure enough, Undella?"

"You're barking up the wrong tree, *Thomas Alva.* I haven't danced since high school, and I can't hardly remember the two-step." She doesn't dare tell him she never danced in high school, either.

"Haven't danced since high school! Where you *been*, girl?"

She shrugs. "Studying to be a bookkeeper. Living with my mama. She was one of *them*," she says, pointing at the church.

"That don't sound like fun. Where's your mama now?"

"At the right hand of the Lord, if *she* has anything to say about it—she died in the spring."

"And your daddy?"

"He died, too, long ago, when I was just going into high school. I *know* that *he's* in heaven. He was good."

Slip gives a sad nod. "You're all by your lonesome here now." It's more an observation than a question.

She gives a shrug. "So my fun's mainly all out ahead of me," she says to change the subject.

"No, it ain't. It's standing right here in front of you. I taught you round the world, I reckon I could get you to remember the two-step. I'm as good a dancer as I am a yo-yo thrower, Stony. You're missing half your life not to dance with me."

"I may be missing it now, but I don't aim to miss it for long. That's what that wall's *for*. Whenever I *do* go to dancing, I don't want Baptists on my mind."

"Only trouble with that is, right *now* is when I'm *here*." He opens his hands out in front of him and rocks back to pose, showing himself off as a prize. "And anyway, about that wall—" he sits back down and shoves his plate to one side, resting his arms flat on the picnic table, heaving a sigh and getting a break-it-gently expression on his face. "I couldn't live with myself if I pulled out of here without talking to you about it."

"What *about* my wall?"

"So far it's fine. It's straight, pretty work. I'm impressed. But—how you going to build it up as high as you want it? You going to lift those rocks up over your head?"

"Of course not," she cries, indignant and relieved. "Do you think I'm a fool that never thought of that? I'm going to build a platform out of wood all the way across, about four foot high! Then I can work the top the same way I did the bottom."

"Well, that's a good plan, all right. But do you know the main rule of stone-wall building?" He waits, but if he thinks she's going to shake her head, he's crazy. She sits there glaring at him. But he goes on anyway. "The higher the wall the broader the base. You've got a nice sturdy three-foot-high wall, I'm not taking nothing away from it. But you didn't start out broad enough." He looks at her, shaking his head, his eyes wide and unblinking, as though trying to hypnotize her. "Not for how high you want to go."

He goes on shaking his head until finally she can't help herself. "How broad does it have to be, according to you?"

"If you made it broad as it has to be for seven feet high, you wouldn't be able to build your platform in front of it because you'd be too far away from the top of the wall to reach over to it. See what I mean? I'm not fooling you, Undella. Seven foot is way high, for a rock wall twelve feet across without no mortar in it. If you didn't do it just right, that thing could fall, one side or the other, and take you or a few Baptists down with it. And then where would you be? Liable or dead, one. I wouldn't have no freestanding seven-foot wall on *my* property. What if some kids tried to climb up it and brought the whole deal over on top of them? And besides, it would take one hell of a heap of stone to build it up seven feet high."

"I get it a little at a time."

"Well, then, I hope you don't mind putting a few more of your dancing years into rock hauling and wall building. You're talking about a long-term project. You could use mortar, but you'd have to take apart all the good work you've already done and start over, with about a million bags of Sakrete." Undella sits with her hands curled into fists in her lap, fat tears welling up in her eyes. "I don't mean to hurt your feelings or spoil your plans. But you don't want to build your wall all out of stone, Undella!" She wants to go over and sit down against it and think about her tall stone idea, rising up straight and perfect with a clear message of mind your own business, like a castle wall, something to look at in and of itself, something to announce to the ones on that side and this that things are going to be different from now on. She gives a rough swipe at her eyes, and he reaches out and touches her arm lightly. "I cry all the time myself, whenever I want to," he says. "It's about the same as laughing, to me. Now, if I was you, I'd just call it done the way it is now. Maybe one more round, to level it off. You *could* finish it out in four-foot boards—that would take you right on up to seven feet, and you'd be done in a day. But if it was me, I'd forget about the Baptists and the wall both, at the same exact minute, which would be this one right now. If they don't like what they see, they got some other directions they can look in, don't they?" He leans over his arm that is still reached across to her on the picnic table, to smile her into his shiny-eyed way of thinking.

And now he stretches behind him and snaps on the radio, and what comes out is that old Sawyer Brown song that used to get her so tickled: "Some girls don't like boys like me—oh, but some girls do." But over the top the organ blares to bring on the offering and she drops down into all the long mornings and evenings she spent inside that pile of red brick trying to feel holiness come over her, squinching up her eyes to pray, trying to bring back the sweet Jesus who was her imaginary playmate when she was four or five, but the more they talked about him, the more he wandered off somewhere to be God.

The older girls would fling off their maroon choir robes that they wore over their outfits and race down the stairs after the service to ambush the boys. There weren't that many Baptist boys, and the girls had to find a husband out of them, so they learned to be quick. Undella didn't give it a try. She couldn't see any Baptist boy she wanted—she couldn't feature herself standing at the back of the church listening to Mrs. Carol Ann Adcock singing "Ah, Sweet Mystery of Life" to get her into the mood to walk up the aisle to become the wedded wife of Scooter MacFee or Earl Wayne Combs. So she just hung up her robe, left the church by the back door, picked her way across the alley, her high heels pricking holes in the warm tar.

At home would be a long afternoon of Sunday dinner, then dishes from Sunday dinner, the radio turned way down low so she could hear something to take the anthem out of her head. Then sitting on the front porch reading a book, looking to see if any of the cars passing by were for her, dream on. She wished she could have been on the basketball team or in the marching band or drama club, but her mama didn't want her going off on those trips she'd heard about. If a neighbor or a relative dropped by, they had cookies and lemonade in the backyard. Or if her mama felt like driving they took a ride, for a big treat. Then homework. Then evening service.

○

She was thinking her life would begin once the wall was finished, but what Slip said is true, that her life is on its own schedule and wants to begin right now.

Slip stands up and spins and tips his hat down over his eyes the way he did when he was fixing to teach her yo-yos. He does a cute chugging motion to the music on the radio. Then he takes hold of some imaginary girl that likes boys like him, one hand around her waist, one holding her hand way up high, and glides her around in a luscious sexy circle, his eyes closed. Then he opens them, and they do double shoot the moons at Undella. He leans down and pulls her up off the bench toward his grin. "This is just get-on-down-into-it dancing," he explains. "Whatever suits you. Freestyle."

She stands there for a minute with him making his sharp finger-snapping moves around her that remind her of a male robin doing his spring dance, asking herself why she put on this silky number if she was just going to stand here like a statue and let him disappear with his yo-yos and his yo-yo secrets and his wall-building expertise and his tall hungry looks. He's going to disappear, that's for sure, but she doesn't see why she should let him do it without dancing with him first, just to see how it feels, because realistically speaking, where's her next chance going to come from? And when it comes (when and if) she wants to know how to act. He goes right on with his dance, crossing one boot in front of the other, snapping his fingers.

So she shakes back all her long thick hair in a bossy way to make up for how bashful she feels around the knees. She taps her foot and holds her elbows close to her and moves the lower part of her arms from side to side to the beat. Slip comes around and gives her a nudge in the small of her back. She squeezes her eyes shut and bends one knee, then the other. Then she opens her eyes a crack and sees he's raised his arms up over his head, and now he's rolling his fists around each other, like he's working the pedals of a bike with them, so she raises up and does that, too. He moves his head like a snake does, side to side. As the song winds down he puts his hand on her waist and turns her three times around, the way they used to do you to play blindman's bluff. On the third turn, she opens her eyes and smiles right into the close face of Slip Finnigan, who could not be a serial killer because he'd be the first one they'd bring in for questioning.

The radio announcer's voice sounds like he's talking out of a muskmelon way down in his gullet. At the same time from across the way comes "The Lord bless you and keep you." The Baptists will be all out in the parking lot in two minutes.

Undella looks at Slip. Slip looks at her. He raises his eyebrows, *what'll it be?* They keep on looking at each other for a few seconds, then she turns around and stacks up what she can carry and he snatches up the radio. They get inside the house, and then they rush around, pulling down shades, laughing high and crazy, while Young Country plays "Way Down Yonder on the Chattahoochee" for about the three millionth time.

"*Now* we need candles," says Slip, rubbing his hands together. "You got any candles laying around, Stony?"

There's about a dozen little fat white ones left over from something at the church last Christmas and a box of tall pink ones, never used, that match her mother's china pattern. They're all in the bottom drawer of the hutch. She gets them out and puts them in saucers and candlestick holders and Fresca bottles, hearing her mama's voice in her head the whole time—"That's right, burn every last candle in the house. And just who do you think is going to scrape all that wax off everything tomorrow?" *Not you, Mama, so don't worry about it,* Undella shoots back, and goes around putting the candles here and there, and Slip comes along after her and lights them. Then he switches off the overhead light and the room is a whole new proposition. He comes along and slides his hand around her back to draw her close, and then he moves her into that slow sad song about falling in love with a dreamer, her face against his chest that she can feel the skeleton of, rising and falling lightly underneath his slippery black shirt. The yellow plastic flowers get mixed up in it—he fixes the lei so that it hangs down the back of him instead of the front.

It doesn't seem much like any two-step, or one-step, either—it's more just standing still and swaying to music, feeling the other one breathe. He's still got on his cowboy hat, his head ducked down toward her, his brown hand that spells "L-O-V-E" cupped around hers, brought up against his shoulder.

Across the alley the cars are starting up, wheeling off, which takes a load off Undella's mind, until the loud knocks start up on the back door. She whips her head up, wild-eyed. Slip just brings her in closer, goes on concentrating on the music. He doesn't even open his eyes. "Undella? Anybody home?" Uncle Chuck calls in a mock-friendly way.

"You don't have to answer that," Slip says then, in a low voice, lips barely moving, still without opening his eyes, as if Uncle Chuck, about the size and shape of a refrigerator, would just disappear like fog.

"He'll walk right in!" Undella whispers back.

"No he won't—I locked the door."

"That won't stop Uncle Chuck. He's got a key! He thinks he owns the place! He thinks I'm his responsibility." She wants to get free so she can run over and switch on the light, but he holds her by the wrist, smiling, shaking his head. "If you touch that light switch, Undella—well, it'll be all over for you."

He looks down at her, smiling mysterious and narrow-eyed under his hat brim.

She stares at him and then at her wrist. "He'll walk in and see all these candles burning and get the wrong idea!" she whispers.

He's not holding her wrist hard; he's just got his thumb and forefinger circled around it like a bracelet. But if she tried to twist her wrist and get free, she's not sure he'd come loose. "Maybe he'll get the right idea," he says, smiling. "Then he'll have to decide what to do about it, won't he?"

"He won't have to decide one thing!" she says, trying to tell him what they're up against in a hurry. "He'll just pick you up by your shirt collar and the back of your jeans and haul you out the front door. I know him."

"No, he won't."

There's another burst of knocking on the back door, this one saying, *I've had just about enough of this, young lady.*

"Yes, he will."

"Listen, Stony. He'd have to get his hands on me first, and I'm kind of your basic greased pig. I know how to duck and dodge and wiggle free. Your Uncle Chuck is a burly man, but he's been standing still where I've been moving. I'm fast on my feet. He couldn't catch me any more than he could catch a fish with his bare hands. And what if he *was* to? Then what's he going to do? Throw me out and sit on the curb all night to keep me from coming back? Sleep in your lounge chair with his shotgun on his knees? He can't do that—that lady in the tight dress wants him home. I'm sure he won't get *her* to camp out here. Besides, he can't stay here forever, and he knows that whenever he clears out, I'll be back." These words set up a slow thrill in Undella.

But she knows her uncle. "He could put you in his car and take you out to the dark country and dump you."

"I doubt he'd talk that lady into riding in the same car with me—she'd be scared I'd disorganize her outfit."

He gives her a look that makes her imagine the disorganized outfits he's left in his trail.

"And even if he dumped me, I'd know how to come back. Sixty, seventy miles is nothing to me."

"Undella!" yells Uncle Chuck, one last time, and then instead of walking in, he stomps down the stairs. They hold still and listen, and pretty soon he's climbed back over the wall and they hear his car start up and turn out of the parking lot.

Slip lets loose of her wrist now. "Is that the uncle that's got the rocks?"

"No, that's Nestor on my daddy's side that's got the rocks. This is Chuck on my mother's side. Oh, I wish I was in a place that didn't have uncles! San Antone or Amarillo or somewhere in the songs."

"You live in Po-duncle," Slip says.

"Po-duncle. You know it, Slip."

"Are there more? We don't want no posse coming along."

They listen to the sound of Uncle Chuck's motor going away. "No. The rest are all aunts."

"Oh, *aunts*," says Slip, grinning. Then he takes her two hands and pulls her in toward him, but the song where Kenny Rogers and Dottie West turn out the light and just hold tight is winding down, and anyway, here comes Uncle Chuck's Caprice back again, around the corner and up the street.

"He's parking it at the front!" she says, and breaks loose from Slip in a panic to look out from behind the edge of the shade. "Yep, it's him," she says, and runs up the hall to lock the front door and shoot the bolt. Slip has come behind her out into the hall. "Go hide out back somewhere," she whispers. "I'll tell him you left a long time ago and I fell asleep."

"It's your life, girl," he says, his hands on her shoulders to get her attention. "You don't have to tell him Lie One. You understand?"

The car door slams and after a minute the trunk lid thuds down, too. "I got to say *some*thing or he'll break down the door to see if I've been murdered and robbed—he's gotten out his tire iron or something. Go on now, Slip."

"Okay, I'm out the back door. I'll be goin' down the alley like a shadow you think you saw but didn't." He slips—there's no other word for it—down the hall and through the kitchen. At the back door, he tips his hat to her, where she's standing now at the front door. "Let me back in, you hear? We haven't got started good on that two-step yet."

"Undella honey, let me in right now!" yells Uncle Chuck. And there goes Slip out the back door, closing it so quiet she can't even hear it, for Uncle Chuck beating on the front door.

Undella takes a deep breath and unbolts it. "Are you satisfied?"

"Are you all right?" Uncle Chuck is wearing his plaid Wednesday sports coat, for Kiwanis and Midweek Service, and he's packing his shotgun. He has a square face with a square gray beard around it. He is flushed up pretty good from all the excitement.

"You breaking down my door to ask me that?"

"Where's that sleazy business?"

"What sleazy business is that?" The shotgun looks slender and dainty in his big red hands.

They're in a standoff, holding each other's eyes with mean looks. "Is he still here?" Uncle Chuck asks, cold and polite.

"You want to bring your firepower in and check?"

"I should have known he'd run off between me being at the back door and at the front." He lets down the shotgun now, disappointed. "What are you *thinking* about, letting that trash in your house? Nobody around here ever saw him before. He'll ruin your good name, and that's just the beginning. What would your daddy say, if he knew this is what his girl's come down to?" Uncle Chuck sings bass in the men's quartet and his voice has a lot of carrying power when he puts his heart behind it.

She steps out onto the porch to keep him from coming in. "You better quit hollering, if you're so worried about my name getting ruined." She doesn't know what her daddy would say. Maybe he'd think Slip Finnigan was a boy after his own heart.

"Why didn't you answer the door before? What were you doing?"

She decides not to tell Lie One. "I was leading my life. I wasn't expecting company."

He looks displeased and dangerous, but then he suddenly shifts gears. "Undella baby," he says, leaning toward her, "you're a girl that's led a sheltered life."

She looked up at half a moon and a clutter of stars over the roofs of her neighborhood. "You're sure right about that. And just how long is a girl that's led a sheltered life supposed to keep on doing it? I'm twenty-one. That's *old*, to still have your damn uncle on the front porch telling you what to do."

"Don't use swears, baby," he says, looking truly pained. "You may be twenty-one, but you're a *young* twenty-one. Your mama, I know how she was, I couldn't hardly talk to her about you. She said she was going to keep you attached at the hip so you wouldn't make the mistake *she* made, falling for your wild daddy. Now look at what's happened. Wild is *one* thing—"

"The mistake *she* made!"

"Well, it was a mistake. We won't try to guess who made it. But listen—someday somebody that's got something to back him up is going to come along. What do you know about where that yo-yo man was before he got to you?"

"Not a thing. That's what I like about him."

He gives his head a slow shake. "You don't have a clue what you're messing with, do you?"

"Maybe I do and maybe it's not what you think."

"Now, I seriously *doubt* it's not what I *think*. I see candles burning, I hear music playing. I see you looking like a tramp in that tacky thing I brought back from Vietnam. How dumb do you think I am?" He gives that snorting kind of laugh she hates. "Nestor's right about you and them rocks—we need to be building a wall around *you*, try to keep the stray dogs away."

"At least that stray dog told me the wall I'm building might fall over on me, which is more than you and Nestor did while he was laughing so hard and you were sadly shaking your head."

She feels hot tears burning her eyes and her hands curling into fists at her side. Making fun of her. Calling her a dog in heat. She wishes she could punch him.

He puts on a tone of trying the best a good-hearted person can to reason with her. "Honey, you got a lot to offer *any*body—a nice little house all paid for, a truck, a good nest egg in that savings account your mama left you." He forgets to throw in her own sweet trampy tacky dog-in-heat self. "Don't you think for a minute he ain't adding it up. You probably look like as close to heaven as a road dog like him is going to get."

She is so mad her eyeballs are throbbing.

But now, words rise up through her anger like a handful of colored balloons. "Why don't you take a leap, Uncle Chuck?" she says lightly, with a crazy smile taking over her face. The words feel very good, like letting a beautiful melody sing out, so she says them again. "Why don't you just take a flying leap?"

He backs his head up in surprise and rebuke. He looks just like Undella's mama, now. Just so grieved she turned out like she did.

He gives a sigh, meaning he's done his best and hit a stump and nobody can blame him. But he's also sad. He sounds sad when he reaches over and gives her a pat on the shoulder. "Well," he says, in his deep, dignified Kiwanis voice. "I can't do anything with somebody that tells me to take a flying leap. Except tell them to hide their cash."

○

After Chuck drives off, Undella stomps through the hall out to the kitchen and starts throwing the dirty dishes into the sink. She slams the pots around. Protect her and back her up. She picks up one thing and then the one next to it, blindly. *Screw you. Fuck off.* She remembers all the good ones people would say in high school. She wishes she'd said one of those instead of *take a flying leap.*

Slip left his sack of yo-yos right in the middle of the kitchen floor. She wants to pick it up and see what it would feel like to sling it over her back and start walking, but she doesn't touch it. It's private property.

Instead, she goes to her bedroom to find the wad of cash she took out of her wall-building pants pocket and left on the dresser this afternoon and forgot about. It's still there. She wishes she didn't feel so relieved. She stands with it in her hand for a minute, then puts the money in her wallet, but leaves her purse hanging on the bedpost, the way she always does. If it turns out that Slip's a robber, then she'll lose what's left of those five twenties after the two yo-yos and the groceries, that's all. She's not going to go hiding things. Either you trust somebody or you don't let them in. She lifts her hair off the back of her neck to cool herself, then goes to her mama's room and finds some lipstick in the top drawer. She leans forward through the dark to put it on, studying herself in the mirror to see if she looks like a tramp. To herself, she looks like a regular good-looking woman. Just not Uncle Chuck's type—too wild. She puts some of the perfume still on the top of her mama's dresser behind her ears. Then she goes to the living room and takes her gold yo-yo out of the top drawer of the marble-top, where she put it away this afternoon, wrapped in white tissue.

She carries it into what used to be the extra bedroom, which she emptied out after her mama died. She didn't want anything hiding the pattern of this carpet, the best in the house. She remembers lying on her belly on it when she was no more than a toddler—it's her earliest memory—trying to see through the roses and bluebirds to whatever was behind them. There's nothing else in the room, not one stick of furniture. It is just big enough to throw a yo-yo in without feeling cramped, high enough to do a round the world without worrying about crashing into a light fixture. She brings in some of the candles, still burning. She throws down the gold yo-yo a few times, to break it in, the way Slip did the green one, until she feels it begin to limber up. Then she starts practicing her tricks. They didn't pull the shades in here, so she can see her reflection going through the motions, and she's thrilled with how her arm in gold silk flashes up and down and here and there, like dancing or doing magic, and then the gold yo-yo flashes out, too, in the direction she sends it. She concentrates on every little flick of her wrist. The more she throws, the more she can feel herself calming down, till there's nothing to her but high hopes and a feeling of how it should feel, even when she messes up. *One of the yo-yo greats*, she says to herself, just to remember who she is and how it sounded for him to tell her that. She's going to call this the yo-yo room, from now on.

She's listening for a knock on the door. She's trying to keep her mind only on the yo-yo, but a picture keeps coming up, of her and Slip, rolling along some leafy back road in her green truck, the bed packed full of yo-yos. The cab windows are rolled down halfway for the morning air. They've got cups of coffee. The sun is just coming up behind them—they're headed west. "All my exes live in Texas," they're singing.

She can't get over how easy it was for her to catch on, how natural it came to her. She thinks about Slip, one trick flashing out after another as though the yo-yo were a bucking bronco with him riding it, trying to hold on, hanging onto his hat. She hasn't a clue how you get that good. She still has to stop after every throw and get her mind around the next one. But the more she throws, the more she feels exactly the same as the yo-yo, brand-new but working out the kinks. She moves through her moves all the way to round the world. She throws one, admiring her reflection in the glass. Then she gets ready and throws another one, and gives a silly-sounding scream because there he is, too, in the reflection—she recognizes him by his hat—standing with the hall light behind him, leaning in the doorway, watching her watch herself. The yo-yo comes back into her hand even though she forgot about it. She never did lock the back door after him, she guesses. He didn't knock, for sure. He just walked down the hall without one sound. She sees him leave the door and come up behind her, and her heart gives a big thud, she doesn't know what of, surprise or fear. She hopes he won't kill her—she doesn't want her last thought on earth to be *Uncle Chuck was right.*

She doesn't turn around. He raises his hands up, standing behind her, as if he's surrendering, or putting a spell on her, looking into the reflection too. Then his hands come down on her shoulders. He says, whispering right in her ear, "You got to loosen up in here." He presses one shoulder, then the other, to drop them down, like some kind of faith healer laying on hands. When he turns her around, he's looking at her the way the yo-yo looks in hesitation waltz—his eyes are two green yo-yos spinning and holding still at the same time, to find out what's next.

"What's next, Stony?" he whispers, drawing the yo-yo string from her finger real slow.

She reaches up and takes his hat off, kneels, and places it carefully on the floor, away from the candles. Then she looks up at him, trying to see if he's going to disappear down the road as soon as he gets all her mama and daddy's money. He's watching her watching him. She runs her fingers up through her hair, hoping it's still stacked up good.

She shakes it back. Something happens then, some slow way he moves down to her, lays his hand on the hollow place behind her collarbone and the underneath of her chin, that makes her sure her twenty self-covered diagonal buttons and her green fire-breathing dragon aren't going to protect her. They've gone over to his side, and somehow, by the same floating way, the bluebirds and the roses now go over to his side, too, and she's thinking, as she slips in and out of not knowing what's her fingers and what's her toes, that she might have to take Uncle Chuck's advice to ask this man that's probably got a girl in every county from Tennessee to Michigan about you-know-what. When her eyes come open to ask, he puts his finger over her lips. "It's all taken care of, honey," he says in a husky, sweet voice. "You don't need to worry. But we might ought to find something to put down here. Something smooth and good-feeling on that pretty skin." So Undella runs in and gets the quilt out of her mama's room—the iridescent satin is worn down to bare threads in places to show the gray batting inside, but the outside color is the same as lake water, or first light in the sky, soft rosy gray. They spread it down the way you spread a blanket for a picnic.

But it's more like being on water.

And he is a man who makes his living spinning things. He's laughing now, right down into her face, and she feels joyfulness rising up from her and zooming into Slip's eyes. The raft is riding on smooth sweet waves, and then the riding part is inside her, and she wonders if she should have told him before now that it isn't just the two-step and yo-yos that she's a newcomer to.

"Are you okay?" he asks. How would *she* know? "Are you okay? Are you okay? I didn't know." He looks worried.

She nods. She doesn't have the words, but she has the actions that speak louder.

"I'm your special occasion," he tells her, lowering his head, laughing down close around her face. "I'm what you've been holding out for."

Later—oh, much later—she rises up over him, her hair hanging down all around his face. "Slip, guess what?" she whispers, in delight. "I got a five-year-old Chevy short-bed."

He stares up at her. "And?" he says, after a few seconds.

"Well—I got the truck. You got the yo-yos and the yo-yo know-how."

He wrinkles his forehead as if she's a problem he can't quite solve, and now he starts in laughing. Every time he tries to stop, off he goes again. He has to sit up and wipe the tears off his cheeks with the heel of his hand.

"What's so funny?" she says, smiling, wanting to join in, but not if she doesn't get the joke.

"Well, lookee there, how good that works out," he says at last, then falls down on his stomach laughing again. "You got the truck. I got the yo-yos. We each got what the other one needs." He puts his arms around her and pulls her down to him again, to show her how true that is. "What you want to do?" he asks, his face right up against hers. "Form a corporation? Where's the dotted line? Sign me up!" He gives her shoulder a little bite. "Hey! We could paint the name of our company on the tailgate. I know—we'll call it *The Good Times Express*. How would that be?"

"That would be good! Listen, Slip, I know you want low overhead," Undella says, trying to talk business. But it seems like everything she says sends him off again.

"Low overhead!" he shouts.

"But see, Slip," she goes on seriously, so he gets his face straightened out. "I'm looking for a business opportunity. We could invest in a whole line of merchandise, not just yo-yos. We could branch out—badminton sets and volleyballs and all sorts of sporting equipment. It would be good to sell somewhere close by the state parks." Once she gets started, she can't make herself stop. "And picture puzzles and poker chips and maybe some board games. Those people stuck in their RVs with two kids have to have something to do when it rains." He's studying the ceiling now, nodding, like a man thinking it over, so she feels she ought to go ahead and lay out the whole thing while she's got his attention. "I'll bet you could clear two hundred dollars a day. We could work out a deal. I've got things to offer—good ideas, business sense. I'd be good at merchandising. And like I say, my truck and a certain amount of capital for the right venture, which I think you might be." She looks at him fair and square.

He looks back. He takes his arm out from around her and leans far back to study her, in a jokey way, like when he rounded the corner and first caught sight of her in her silk pajama top. He reaches out for his hat. He gets it by the crown and lifts it onto his head, bends the tip to an angle that pleases him. He grins at her, from underneath the brim.

"You could still go off on your own," she said. "I'd meet up with you somewhere we agreed on. And you could give me yo-yo lessons, and maybe someday I could sell, too—while you were walking out one end of a state, I could be hitting the spots you weren't going to get to."

He takes off his hat again and slings it clear across the room, then brings her in close to him. "There ain't no spots I'm not going to get to," he says in his husky, lady's-man voice.

○

He's dead asleep and doesn't stir. His arm is thrown up over his eyes. She loves his arm, especially the underneath of it, where it's purely a fish, no mermaid, a green and blue bass, jumping for joy up from his wrist to the inside of his elbow. She goes to her bedroom and puts on her pink chenille bathrobe, then comes back and lies down again, turning on her side, resting her head on her hand. Without his hat, his green eyes closed, he looks almost as young as she is. The magic and glitter of him have drifted off, more in the air now than in him. Asleep, he looks like he never had a mama. Lost in his face, and in his tall bony body, so sharp and definite and fast and knowing about what's what when it's moving around, but asleep, all sorrowful ribs and shoulders.

It makes her so sad for him that she gets up and goes into the kitchen to fix him some plum cobbler, with ice cream on top.

She's weak-kneed and running a fever. Coming down with something, ha ha. Like she's sunburned all over. She puts her bare foot out and touches the burlap sack, still there by the kitchen table. Sleazy business. Road dog. That's Uncle Chuck's way of talking about what he doesn't understand. Most people don't want to be too swept off their feet. Most people don't trust magic as much as Undella does. It messes up their idea of how the world runs.

But Undella likes it. She feels it in the air all around her, great billows of magic rising up, changing where she is, her mama's kitchen with the same old refrigerator and sink and iron skillets and pie safe, into somewhere she never saw before. *Here I am*, she says to herself, watching her hand with an old spoon in it scooping ice cream, and her life feels like the silver edge cutting down, scooping deep into what those three delicious words amount to. The picture of the two of them going down the road together comes into her mind again, and her vision of the future shines through, as if it has always been there, but hidden by a fog that is now burning off.

It's going to be good!

She takes the bowl of cold ice cream and warmed-up cobbler into the room where Slip is sleeping and also another warm quilt to draw over him as the night cools off. She puts the cobbler down on the floor beside him and goes back to her own bedroom to collect pillows to put between him and the wall when he sits up. She spreads the quilt over him—he nestles down into it like a baby, and she slides down under it beside him again. He pulls her close up against him without opening his eyes. "I brought you something good to eat," she whispers, not certain whether she ought to wake him.

"Feed it to me," he whispers back, with his eyes still closed.

"Okay." She reaches over to the other side of him—he grins and catches her by both arms. She laughs out a laugh that startles her with how deep and comfortable it sounds and says, "Wait, now, Slip." She picks up the bowl, fixes a spoon that's half cobbler and half ice cream. He still hasn't opened his eyes. "Open your mouth," she orders and, when he does, she feeds him like a baby.

He smiles, his mouth moving the way a baby's does over something new that is unbelievably delicious, paying attention, face full of joy that is close to crying.

"I'll fix the pillows so you can sit up."

He pushes himself into a sitting position, still with his eyes closed.

"Wait!" she says, getting another idea, and she runs back into the kitchen for the Hershey bar. She unwraps it, hurrying back down the hall to him, gone back to sleep sitting up, his hands clasped on his chest. She breaks off a small piece of chocolate. "Open your mouth," she says again. She lays the chocolate on his tongue.

At first he draws back, and then he begins to get the taste. He moves it around in his mouth. It reminds her of Communion. He smiles, then swallows. "You're full of surprises, ain't you."

She wishes she had other things—peach brandy, tapioca pudding, strawberries—to feed him. Instead, she gives him a kiss. He opens his green eyes then. "Undella, Undella," he says, as if memorizing her. "Undella Undella Undella."

Then he says, "What time is it? Don't tell me it's morning."

"It's some time of night I never heard of."

"Well, good then." He draws her up against him with one arm, settles the bowl in his lap, arranging every bite carefully, with just the right amount of ice cream.

She wishes she could go out and buy him some new walking shoes. And a nice knapsack. And a belt buckle with "TAF" engraved on it.

"You are an out-of-sight woman," he says. "And you don't even know it." And then he's asleep. She sits up looking at him for a while, and then she goes to sleep, too.

○

The next time she wakes up, there's sun all over the carpet, another beautiful day, and no wall to build! A wall's a wall from both sides, she's just now figuring out. She's given up the whole idea, overnight. It makes her feel light. Light-headed. She'll leave it the way it is, just haul off the loose rock and get the grass to grow back. She thinks there may come a time when she's shut of Baptists altogether. Her future's up in the air. *Up in the air*, she says to herself. *A flying leap*, she says.

And now it comes to her that she's here on the grayish-purple eiderdown all by herself.

She gets up and goes out to the kitchen. "Slip?" she calls, but her heart isn't in it. The empty silence answers back. The sack of yo-yos is gone. She ties up the sash of her pink bathrobe. Slippery Slip has slipped. Skipped out. She's not even going to get Lesson Two.

All his sweetness comes back down over her, his long wrists, his legs meant for traveling, his pulse she could see in the blue vein into his jaw. She sits down, forsaken, lonely, at the kitchen table. She doesn't want to feel this weepy sorrowful way but once.

Well, she thinks, wiping her eyes with the sleeve of her bathrobe, she took her chances. She knew the whole time that what she was messing with was, like he said, a special occasion. Her magic time. Once in a lifetime doesn't often turn into twice. Good-bye to her dream of seeing the country with Slip Finnigan beside her in her truck. Good-bye to *The Good Times Express.*

"Uh-oh," she says then, and she runs down the hall to her bedroom. Her purse is where she put it, hanging on the bedpost. Her money is still there, in her wallet where she stashed it.

What is not there is the ring with her truck keys on it.

She barrels back down the hall and barefoot out the back door, down the steps and across the stone path to the garage. "No, no, no," she's saying, rolling up the door, waiting for the first sight of her truck to make her laugh at this sick prickly feeling traveling up through her gut. But there's nothing in the garage to laugh about but an old oil stain in the concrete slab from her mama's Impala. Her green truck is as gone as a truck can be, her beautiful Chevy short-bed. High whimpering sounds are coming out of her. "Stole my truck," she whispers out loud, holding onto the side of the garage, afraid her knees are going to give out. Her heart is pounding so hard she hears it. Her truck is traveling eighty miles an hour away from her, right now, down highways she doesn't even know about. Two big hiccupping sobs escape her. The truck she paid eighty-five hundred for, two and a half months ago. The truck that was her ticket out of here, if she'd only known it sooner. If she'd been able to imagine *out of here* on her own.

Slip Finnigan, Slip Finnigan, and all he did—she bends over double, clutching her stomach. All *she* did. Feeding him that Hershey bar. And him taking it. A wave of dark rage goes over her. Squeezing her eyes shut, gritting her teeth, she sees his bloody forehead crashing through the windshield, and that white sleazy flea-market hat way on down the road. But she takes it back—it hurts her worse to think of something happening to her truck, even if she never will see it again, than to think about him stealing it.

And now what in the world is she going to do? Call the police and turn herself into the laughingstock and fool of all the town? "And when was this fellow last seen, Miss Jones?" Call Uncle Chuck and tell him he was right all along? *Right right right*, the air is ringing with it. Everything her uncle said last night out of his square face.

She'd rather take the loss. Swallow it down, like a piece of broken glass. It's hers.

As Slip Finnigan well knew the whole time. *Pretty lady.* He probably didn't even especially want to lie down with her—this sharp terrible thought stabs into her chest. He just wanted to get some insurance she wouldn't tell on him. That's probably what he meant by *out-of-sight woman*. Soon to be.

And you don't even know it, he said. She knows it now. She's lucky not to be more out-of-sight than she is. She's lucky he didn't kill her.

She starts to roll the garage door back down—to hide from the nosy world how completely disappeared is the truck she paid half her Mama's savings for back on May 23rd—as something flashes yellow and catches her eye: a ray of sun has landed on his string of plastic flowers, draped over the top of her iron digger.

She stands for a minute staring at it, feeling him in the air all around her. She can see him, for a minute, rolling the garage door open a few inches at a time so as not to make any noise, then getting into the truck, taking off the emergency brake, letting the truck roll on back as far as it would, then getting out and closing the garage door the same careful way he opened it, hoping to buy himself another hour or two before she discovered she'd been robbed. But before he did, as much of a hurry as he was in, he took off that lei and hung it there for her to find.

Then he jumped back into the cab and turned the key and backed out onto the street fast, headed toward Highway 62, the possibilities of life in front of him, the starry sky dark blue and secret above him, his brown hands on the wheel.

While she was still dead to the world, with a smile on her face.

She wanders a few steps back into the darkness of the garage, drawn by the shining yellow, as though it held some mystery. When did he take the keys, she wonders suddenly. When he went in to wash up before dinner? Was he planning the whole time he was eating her food and dancing with her and then on through the night, through all his sweet smiles and touches, to steal her truck? No wonder he laughed so hard when she offered to *give* it to him, more or less.

From the time she asked for a lesson, he was figuring what he could get off of her. A chicken dinner, and then he'd see.

No. He was planning all along to slip off, but he *didn't* plan to take the keys. It was just an impulse, a bad habit he couldn't break. He'd already seen her purse, and couldn't help making that small detour as he was on his way out. It takes all her energy and makes her tired to imagine that a person who was so nice about her wall and her cooking and her yo-yo mistakes could turn around and be a thief. She probably put it into his mind by all her mouthiness about investment opportunities. And now he's driving along knowing he shouldn't have done it. He's about to turn around and drive on back, and give her a lecture about how he stole her wheels as a warning to her to be more careful.

No. She isn't going to hold out any hope on that. By now, even if he wanted to turn back, he must know he'd stand a chance of driving right up on an investigation into grand larceny. He wouldn't do any good at all in jail. Once he fired that truck up, there wasn't anywhere to go but straight on.

Anyway, he didn't take her house keys, or her cash money. She doesn't know why. She's not going to put it down to friendship. Maybe he only took what he couldn't keep himself from taking.

The empty cool darkness inside the garage spins around her head, but there's something heavy and flat inside of her. He took the keys first thing. She knows it. He knew the whole time—the whole time!—just what he was going to do. She puts her hands over her face for the shame of it.

He won't be back. Not ever. He is the Yo-Yo Man, Slip Finnigan. What was she thinking about, trying to make him into a small business? He's gone, and so is her green truck, which was sitting here all this time waiting for her to want to go where it wanted to take her. Not to Uncle Nestor's for another load of rocks. Oh no! Some entirely other direction, somewhere in the songs. But she was too ignorant, too new at it, to imagine anywhere she didn't already know, and she didn't know anywhere but Uncle Nestor's.

She sees that there's a narrow strip of torn paper stuck into the plastic flowers on the iron digger. She pulls it out. Written on it, in fat dark pencil, is "1-800-777-YOYO. Love, Slip Finnigan."

That isn't even his name. Thomas Alva, either. He made *that* one up while she was sitting there looking at him. Still, he's not so smart. She could give this piece of paper to the police and they could catch him, even without his real name. Didn't he think of that when he left it for her?

He knew she wouldn't call in the law.

She puts the number in the pocket of her bathrobe. She takes the plastic lei off the iron digger, turns it through her fingers. She tells herself she's going to keep it as a reminder of what a fool she was, a reminder of how hateful and false the world can be. But that isn't quite it. She wants it because she wants it. She hesitates, then puts it around her neck, pulling her hair up over it. She likes the bright yellow color against her petal-pink robe. She pulls down the garage door, goes back into the kitchen, listening to how everlasting the air is in here. "He stole my truck," she says out loud once more. Her voice this time sounds flat and final. No whimpers in it. And that wasn't all he stole—in a jumble on the empty-room floor are the eiderdown and the Hershey Bar wrapper and her jeans and dragon pajama top. And all through the house are the burned-down Sunday school candles, pools of hard wax in every saucer.

No—except for the truck, he didn't take anything she didn't freely give. And he showed her a good time. It wasn't worth a good-as-new Chevy short-bed, but it was pretty good.

And he taught her the fundamentals of yo-yos. He was lying, like as not, when he told her she could be a yo-yo great. But still, she wants to keep on practicing.

She feels the house's air seeping into her every time she breathes. She's hanging onto that lei of plastic flowers as if it might keep her from falling a long empty way.

"Listen!" she tells herself, since there's nothing anywhere around here to tell it *to* her. "You *are* an out-of-sight woman. Just watch."

She lights the fire under the coffeepot. Her movements feel heavy and grim, but her brain is clicking. Her lips are pressed tight, as she peels off a couple of slabs of bacon, but something's coming to her. A plan. First, she's going to throw out everything in the refrigerator, the leftover chicken and cobbler and all, and clean up the house. Then she's going to walk down to E-Z Terms Used Cars. Hunter Wurley says that he'll always treat her right, as a memorial to her father. She'll buy whatever he'll sell her for somewhere under a thousand dollars, and buy it fast. She'll tell him something or other—that she needs a nice old car to go along with her truck, nothing special, just something for when she wants to tool around with her many friends, but good for another twenty thousand miles, say. When the deal is done, she'll come back and pack. She wants to be gone before Uncle Chuck shows up—late this afternoon, is what she figures. She'll have to leave him a note of some kind to keep him from getting the police in on it. "Have gone off for a vacation from all the free advice. Don't worry—the Yo-Yo Man is not with me. I'll call in a day or so. P. S. I guess you could say I'm taking a flying leap myself. Ha! Ha!" Undella lets the start of a smile out onto her lips at that. On the way out of town, she'll go by the bank to draw out enough of what's left of her mama's money to get herself down the back roads and through all the towns, small and large, till she finds one she likes the look of, Austin, San Antonio, Albuquerque! The names ring like bells. She's not particular what she does when she gets there—maybe she could drive a UPS truck! She's going to need a paycheck coming in.

Once she's got her feet under her, she'll put her mama's house on the market. She'll come back and turn the place out, sell all the Depression glass and chifforobes and dresser scarves right out in the front yard. She doesn't want anything but the rug with roses and bluebirds in it.

She thinks about laying for Slip Finnigan at the Mt. Sterling Post Office—he probably had a new shipment coming in there—but he'd be too smart to pick it up, she thinks. He's in Louisville or Ashland by now, looking to get a river or two between him and her. And what would she do, anyway, if she *did* spot him? Yell for the police? Run him over with her clunker? Face him out and tell him she wouldn't press charges if he'd hand over the keys? He said he was fast on his feet and she believes him. She'd be wasting her time. It would kill her to see him swinging down the sidewalk on the prowl for the next old girl to charm the pants off of—but why would he want to push his luck? He's already had the biggest fool in Kentucky.

She's not going to think about it any more. She's got her own plan to work out. She means to drive off and leave all the people who knew her in her plaid days. The old tick, tick of the kitchen clock. The half-built wall. Her vision of the future still holds: she wants to see the country, only not with Slip Finnigan. And not in her truck that was her most prized possession. She hopes whatever old wreck Hunter Wurley unloads on her will hold up long enough to get her to somewhere good. Once she gets there, she's got her quick wits and business sense to rely on. She still has assets—what's left in the bank, and this house here and all its contents. *The Good Times Express* might yet roll. Maybe, by the time the house sells, she'll know something good to do with her money.

She'll go on practicing yo-yos, getting better and better, in her free time when she's not driving the UPS truck. One day when she least expects it, she'll call the yo-yo number. When her yo-yos come in, she'll carry them out to some state park or campground near wherever it is she ends up. She'll start throwing double walk the dogs, her green yo-yo in one hand, her gold in the other. Maybe a crowd will start forming.

And when she's got them interested, when she's got them where she wants them, she'll lay her round the world on them. Whoosh! Zing! She'll give them a show.

She thinks she can do it. She's a natural for the sport. She's a born athlete.

BANANA BOATS

The old days, the Chicago days, rooms full of the smell of chicken *paprikás*, coffee, roasting pork, simmering prunes and apricots. Dark rooms full of dark furniture, of horsehair, claw feet, doilies, crucifixes with palm fronds stuck behind them. Of trunks and chests that women opened—neighbors, aunts—and took things out of: lace collars wrapped in tissue, smelling of lavender, tea towels, starched and ironed, with crocheted edging, tiny vases of pink crystal, stroked, admired, offered. *Here. For your hope chest.*

Dark, crowded rooms, three slept in one bed. Everyone so poor, and yet there was always something to give, always something on the stove. Enough to feed anyone who came, even if it was just soup made with tomatoes and onions and dandelion greens from the park, or tripe, sliced very thin, fried with eggs. Always money for a handful of cigarettes, always music, Irving Berlin, Sigmund Romberg—"Come, come, I love you only, come, hero mine." Carl the tenor, Joey the baritone, Frank the bass. Oh, Rosa could sing, in those days! She was the alto, she knew the harmonies. They all knew them. The old gang. Now, in the middle of Florida, sixty years later, her voice was a thin four-noted reed. She tried it testingly, had to clear her throat and start again. "Lay your head upon my pillow." Rosa liked the sad songs, with the beautiful melodies, the songs about knowing it was over. Marty Robbins, her favorite, dead now, she couldn't believe it.

She watched her hands coming up out of the soapsuds. Her mother's hands came to her: down in the washtub, fishing through the water for the next shirt to scrub on the board. Thick palms, broad nails—strong hands, made for work, like her own, stretching to get around all the strings of the mop. Smelling of onions or bleach, when she lifted Rosa's face to give her a kiss.

Father Novatny, tall, with long eyes like a saint's, gray-blue—he wanted to leave the Church to marry Rosa's mother! But she wouldn't let him. It was supposed to be a secret, but Genevieve knew somehow, because she was the oldest, sixteen, and she told Emma and Agnes. Agnes told Rosa, who was only nine, too young to hear such things, Emma said—Agnes got a smack for telling. When the news came out that Father Novatny had asked to be transferred to another diocese, Agnes and Rosa ran and sat down on the steps of the church, hugging each other and crying, waiting for him to come with tears in his eyes to say good-bye to them. *Such beautiful girls*, they thought he'd say. *Good-bye, take care of her for me.* They kept themselves in tears for an hour, out there in the cold, but Father Novatny never showed up.

Rosa rinsed each dish and put it in the rack. Two plates, two forks, a pot. Two mugs. Things got simpler and simpler, a bowl of cornflakes for breakfast, a sandwich for lunch, then *Days of Our Lives*.

Only today, they didn't watch.

"Buried alive," Gilbert had said, at the end of lunch, standing by the chair, rattling his keys in his pocket as if he wasn't sure what he would do next. The next time she saw him he was headed out the door in his Bermuda shorts and no shirt. "Where are you going, in this heat?"

"To *work*, Rosa."

He used to call her his ball and chain, just kidding, a long time ago.

When she was twelve, thirteen, she would go with her mother sometimes to measure the rich Bohemian women out in Cicero for corsets. She would watch her mother working over their stout figures with her thin, flashing tape measure, gossiping with them in the old language, laughing with them in her dark way that made Rosa think she was saying something that wasn't too nice, holding the heel of her hand under her breast. She would call out the measurements for Rosa to write down in the book. Then they would all have coffee and *kolache* in the parlor.

Rosa's brothers and sisters in Chicago, the few still alive, could carry on a conversation in Bohemian yet, swearing and insulting each other's big behinds. She forgot, no one to talk it with down here, what little she ever knew. It seemed that what stayed were the dirty words and the words to a few songs. "*Ty to musís platiti.*" That was the one about the bad boy Pepichek stamping on the cabbages in the garden of Anninika, and she says, "You! You must pay for this!" A merry tune, like a polka, for such words.

She went into the bedroom, creased the down pillows once, lengthwise, with a slap of her forearm, so that they would sit in a perfect roll along the headboard. *Lay your head upon my pillow, Hold your warm and tender body close to mine.* She smoothed the counterpane toward the head of the bed, banging all the wrinkles up under the pillows.

Her brain felt like that. Smooth.

Gil was still out there, edging the driveway, to teach her a lesson, his bare chest dripping with sweat. An old man now. He looked like a baby boy, just learning to walk, teetering along, chin down, dragging the edger, his little behind poked out.

Ninety-eight degrees out there. Let him do what he wants.

Sometimes she felt she lived in a deep, smooth-sided place now. Something like a well. Way up above her, people talking. Gil telling his stories, trying to get attention. Not from her. She'd heard enough stories from him already.

She turned and looked out the window again. *I see London I see France.* Gil, lying on his back now in the grass, his thin legs sticking out the wide holes in his Bermuda shorts—she could see all the way to his white BVDs, a little shine up there in the dark. He made a *V* with the edger, which lay across the driveway. It came to her then that he might be dead, a new idea. It sent her flying back down the hall and out the front door. She was kneeling beside him, her hand on his wet, closed face.

It looked closed forever. She heard a thin sound—a high hum she was making up in her head. She saw her life, her life alone, a thin white sheet on the line, blowing and bellying out and snapping in the wind.

But when she saw his eyelids flutter, heard his little fake moan, the sheet stopped flapping, hung still. She thought, coldly, *Oh, this one knows how to flutter his eyelids; he knows how to moan.* Pretending to be dying, she'd given him the idea by telling him to kill himself. Ninety-eight degrees and he's out there edging the driveway, not even wearing his baseball cap. "It *needs doing*, Rosa." Giving a lecture. The small foot in the white sneaker stepping down on the edger, to show it always did everything right. "Stay out here, then. Kill yourself, if it makes you happy," she told him.

It made him happy. Pretending to be at death's door. He loved death's door. He knew how to get there, and get back.

What if she just turned around and left him there to give his brain a sunbath until he felt like coming in? *Just turned around and left him there.* She saw herself for a second backing the car down the driveway, right over the edger. At first she couldn't see why not. But then the idea made a flutter in her chest, like a bird with sharp wings trapped behind her ribs. Where would she go? She was staying. Let *him* go, if that's what he wanted.

Anyway, he didn't look too good—maybe he really did pass out, a little heat stroke maybe.

She stooped behind him and got him lifted into a sitting position, laid his arm around her shoulder, and pulled him to his feet, her arms slipping up his wet back. She wasn't calling anyone for help—a big occasion, an audience, just what he wanted. She dragged him across the grass, the heat around her legs like thick water. One foot, then the other, up the three concrete steps and the last hard one, over the threshold into the air conditioning. He sagged against her across the rug, moaning.

Putting on, always putting on, she thought, and then, *Bastard.* Heart attacks, fainting spells. All her life she was waiting for the next time his eyes rolled back in his head. The trouble was, back at the beginning, it was nothing to joke about, a lot of doctors at Johns Hopkins agreed. You never knew when he was going to keel over. But his heart had healed itself a long time ago, the way they said it would, if he lived long enough, only by then he was used to the excitement. He couldn't break the habit. She got him to the couch, lowered him, put pillows under his feet. The whole side of her was wet with his sweat. He opened his blue eyes, pretending he didn't know where he was. They had a sliding icy look.

"You passed out from the heat," she told him. He closed his eyes again, to show he wasn't pleased with what she said. What she was supposed to say was, "Oh Gilbert, you were right. This yard's too much for us now."

She hurried to the kitchen for a basin of warm water, brought it back, knelt, and sponged him off. Let him hire somebody to take care of the yard. He had plenty of money. Enough to buy a condominium was enough to hire somebody to take care of the yard. He lay there like a corpse in his folded brown skin. Maybe he really did faint, he could have gone that far. Maybe he'd just as soon die as stay here, buried alive. She got him a glass of water, raised his head. "Cold," he said, in a cranky voice. She wiped the water that had trickled down onto his chest, ran into the bedroom to get a blanket, came back and covered him, then straightened herself and looked at him, his brown hand laid out on his chest in a dainty way—wrist up, fingers spread. When she'd gone out before to try to make him come in, he'd said, "You want to stay in this house but you have no *idea* what's involved." No *ah*dyuh, that was how he pronounced it. "Out in that heat," she told him now. "Anyone would pass out." He closed his eyes. Pretty soon he was snoring.

The clock went off on the marble-topped chest. It had the same tune as Big Ben. She didn't know how to make it stop chiming. She pulled out the chest and unplugged it, so it wouldn't disturb Gilbert. Let it be 2:25 forever, it was okay with her. But she felt guilty—the kids had given it to them for their golden, a couple of months back. It was made the same year she and Gilbert got married, Tom told her—one of the first electrics. "Don't remind me, kiddo," she said. "I'm one of the first electrics myself." When it stopped buzzing and clicking around, the silence came down in the house. The hum of the refrigerator was the only thing. Except the mocker in the oak tree, and Gilbert snoring quietly.

She'd been trying all day to remember the name of the President of the United States. She went down the alphabet, hoping a letter would jog her memory of the President's name. *A, B, C. C* was Carter—she remembered Jimmy Carter and his nice wife strolling down the street, hand in hand.

"Your mother's first response to everything is no," Gilbert told the kids. Ball and chain. It hadn't always been no. Back at the beginning, for a long time it was *yes, yes, yes,* dumb her, like a song. From the heart. Lunchtime, sitting there eating his cookie, sharp little chews, jaw popping. Then, "I'm buying. You can come if you want to. I'm not going to let you bury me alive, Rosa."

She put a chicken in the pot, for soup. That would be good for him, with carrots and parsley and noodles. She started a load of laundry, looking out across the backyard. They'd planted those live oaks, the tallest in the neighborhood now, when they moved in. Stephen was a baby here, out in the yard in his little green bathing suit, pulling up zinnias, putting them in milk bottles. A wonderful baby. He would get so quiet when you sang him a sad song. *On a mountain stands a lady, who she is I do not know.* That was one of them. *All she wants is gold and silver, all she wants is a fine young man.*

All these years—half her life. She could take care of the yard herself, rake the leaves, weed the beds. She liked to do it. In the evenings, when it was cool.

She went into the bathroom and got her savings book out from under the stack of single sheets. Over $20,000 in there now, from the rent money on the garage apartment. Just in case. She'd started putting it away that time when he cheated on her. She had her Social Security, too. She didn't think he could sell the house without her consent—*her* name was on the deed, too, she knew that much.

This condominium business, all it was was boredom—not even boredom, just wanting something new to talk about, some new way to get attention, something important to do—sort through things, make lists, follow her around saying, Rosa, we *must* do this, and Rosa, we *must* do that.

She wanted nothing, to be quiet, smooth. No wrinkles for words to hide in, *bastard, dirty two-timer*, she didn't want those words anymore. Or the other ones that always came rushing in afterward, guilty conscience—*loving father, good times, the bad with the good, you've made your bed*. She was sick of her own words; they tired her out. "Such are the vicissitudes of life." That was what Tom used to say in high school, to be funny. She liked to say it, liked the sound of the words, the way they brought trouble down to size, made fun of it.

She remembered only the old days, not the name of the President. What would happen to her if Gilbert left? She didn't think he would do it. *He won't*, she told herself. *He can't*. She wasn't sure whether he could or not. "Go then," she had told him. He gave her a fast sharp look, and then started nodding, in a sarcastic way. "As usual, you don't have the *faintest* notion what you're talking about. I couldn't buy a condominium without selling this place."

This place, he said, as if he hated it.

She was pretty sure her name was on the deed.

He didn't wake up. She kept tiptoeing in to check on him, hoping he would stir, but he slept on, on his back, as the room got darker, his mouth fallen open. Finally, Rosa changed into her nightgown, ate some soup, and watched a program on whales. How they sang to each other from afar. The lonely songs seemed to come from their bellies, from their big hearts.

When the program was over, she went in and laid her hand against Gil's forehead. It was only a little warm. He breathed in and out peacefully. She covered him to the chin, turned out all the lights.

She crawled up onto the high mattress and looked at her short bowed legs, brown against the sheet where her waltz-length nightgown ended. "Ride 'em, cowboy!" That's what the boys in Chicago yelled at her, that summer after third grade, when she finally got nits and had to have her head shaved. A wool stocking cap, all summer.

The bad boys would chase her, trying to pull it off. She learned to run fast. "Ride 'em, cowboy," they yelled after her. Once Teddy Starcheski caught her. He said he wouldn't pull her cap off if she would give him a kiss. She pretended she would, but when he leaned toward her, she kicked him hard in the shin and ran like crazy up the sidewalk to her house, shrieking all the way.

When Gilbert was better, when he was in a good mood, he would make up a story about what had happened this afternoon, for the neighbors, or his poker club. He would tell it in his flirty voice, how she came out and threw him over her shoulder and dumped him on the sofa. She tried to think it was funny, what had happened. *Such are the vicissitudes.* She thought how she would listen to him telling his story, how she would roll her eyes up at the ceiling and say, so everyone would think she was kidding, "I should have left him right where he fell. He had it coming."

"You'll keep me buried alive until I die," he had said this morning. Coming to her with his brochures and booklets. Pool and patio. Bridge club, Spanish lessons. "And what would I do?" she asked. "Stay in my five rooms and rot?" She wasn't the right one for him. Maybe once she was, but no more, not for a long time, face it. He needed somebody more like himself. Yes, and don't worry, he'd *gotten* somebody more like himself. Two-timer—she'd found out, never mind how, but that was over now, and now it was something else, sell the house they'd lived in thirty-five years, all paid for, and move to a condominium so he could play bridge all day with the rich Presbyterian widows—here they come with their one-dish casseroles and their nice cotton dresses.

He'll kill me yet, she said to herself.

But Dr. Jordan wanted to know, later, on the telephone, if she was trying to kill *him*. When she called him, after she woke up in the middle of the night and found Gilbert on the bathroom floor. "Are you trying to kill him, Rosa?" Dr. Jordan asked. "Why didn't you call me the first time he passed out?"

She heard her voice, like a runaway horse with the cart still hitched on, explaining and explaining.

"From now on, when he faints, call me," Dr. Jordan interrupted her crossly. "He's eighty-two years old, you know."

He sent an ambulance. Two men carried Gilbert out of the house on a stretcher. Something about this rang a bell, as though on a stretcher was where Gilbert was always supposed to be. They didn't have the light flashing, too bad—if Gilbert had his way, there would be a siren and a crowd of neighbors standing around in their bathrobes with worried expressions, telling each other, "It's Gil Cannon. Something's happened to Gil."

She followed behind the ambulance in her car, around the lake, fast, praying not to hit something.

By the time she got to his room, they had him hooked up to a machine. He was a small man—a miniature Ike, that's who everyone always used to say he looked like. He let out some weak gurgling moans. "Out in the hot sun all afternoon, edging the driveway. He wouldn't stop," she explained to Dr. Jordan and the nurses. "Sweat pouring off of him. It didn't even need it." The nurses looked at her, then away. Maybe she had already said that, maybe she was talking too loud. Or maybe the nurses were mad at her, too. "I think he had a little heat stroke." She stood at the foot of the bed, not knowing what to do, while the nurses bustled around. Then, out of the blue, the banana boat came into her mind. *Tampa to Rio.* She hadn't thought about it in years. A hiccup of laughter rose in her chest. She bit her cheeks, looked down at Gilbert, in that white hospital gown, his dry lip caught on his eyetooth, his eyes rolled back, just slits of white showing under the lids. That only made it worse. She had to turn away, had to squeeze her eyes shut and pretend to be choking, because Dr. Jordan and the nurses already thought she was crazy.

She wasn't the crazy one.

"I want you to go on home, Rosa," Dr. Jordan said. He put his hand on her shoulder. "We'll run some tests tomorrow to make sure, but I don't think there's anything much wrong with him, besides being dehydrated." *So give him a drink of water*, she thought, but she said, "I want to stay for a while." To make up for everything.

"Suit yourself," he said, smiling his thin smile, patting her shoulder, trying to be nice.

She sat in the chair in the dark corner, out of everybody's way. Just nerves. She wiped her eyes now, in private. She remembered how she and her friend Josephine used to bite their cheeks to keep from laughing in church. How they would kneel, their red faces hidden in their hands, how they would weep and sometimes wet their pants, their shoulders helplessly shaking as the priest waved the censer.

She and Josie, strolling down the street arm in arm, harmonizing. "We'll build a sweet little nest/Somewhere out in the West." What was west of Chicago? Don't ask *them*. All they knew was which boys liked them. Counting them off on their fingers, like beads on the rosary. Putting flowers behind their ears and waltzing together. Josie's mother had beautiful black hair down to her knees when she took out the pins to brush it. No gray at all, until she was sixty. Ma Kish. She made them *dobos torte*, ten thin layers, with whipped cream filling in between. "Eat, or you'll never fill out."

Dancing the Varsouviana down through the dark rooms of the Kishes' railroad flat, Ma Kish rolling out the wild chords on the old upright.

On laundry day, she and Josie would dress up in the dusty organdy curtains and pretend they were princesses, or brides. The smell of soap and steam in the little flat, and they would be back in Ma Kish's dark bedroom, arranging the ruffled edging of the peach-colored curtains around their heads and shoulders, helping themselves to the rouge, looking at themselves in the big mirror with the gilt frame around it, hardly believing their eyes.

One of the nurses—the one with the suntan and green eyes—came in and gave Gilbert a shot, then quickly arranged him again with the covers over him. His eyelids fluttered; then he was asleep. The nurse looked at him, head to one side. "What a little doll," she said. She looked at Rosa as if to tell her she ought to appreciate him more, take better care of him.

She wished she could make him wake up and tell the nurse how he came down with yellow fever after the banana boat got to Brazil, since she was so interested. How the natives carried him out of the jungle in a hammock on poles, and he screamed and screamed, out of his head. Rosa remembered his clear, serious blue eyes when he told her, to explain why he put his hand over his chest like that sometimes, how near death he had come that time, and so young. Holding her hand: *the fever scarred my heart, Rosa*. She wondered what this pretty young nurse would do with someone who held her hand and told her that, with such a sad look. What *Rosa* had done, of course, was marry him.

She was twenty-four by then, not so bad these days, but old, an old maid already, in those times, bringing presents to Josie's two little boys, Chuckie and Dennis. Getting sad. Rosa went into an empty church one evening after work and prayed God to send her someone to take care of. Two weeks later, God sent Gilbert, with his scarred heart and thin overcoat. Sent him to the Aragon Ballroom, sent him across the polished floor to ask her to dance. Wayne King playing "Always," the sweet clarinet sliding its narrow notes into the smoky air. She had on her new crimson dress, long-waisted. "Your name should be Rose, in that dress," he said, his voice not like any voice from around Chicago. "It's Rosa," she told him, feeling shy, because of the nice way he put his hand on her waist. He told her she was a wonderful dancer. She knew she was a wonderful dancer, but she was twenty-four, a supervisor at the telephone company, making good money, even in the Depression, because she had worked there by then for ten years. She lied about her age to get that job, the only lie she ever told.

He held her just the way a new man should, respectful, lightly sliding his hand—smooth and dry, not sweaty, like some—over hers; she felt, in his arms, that she could leave all the steps to him. She hardly knew she was dancing. Something was going to happen, something was happening. She relaxed, her brow finally resting against the sweet clean side of his neck. Her dreams would come true, she should relax.

A Southerner, so courteous, new in town. "Where are you from?" "From far away." *A true gentleman*, her sister Emma said. It was a cold, snowy winter. He'd found a job as a shoe salesman, and he was grateful to have it, he told her. He'd lost everything in the Florida Bust. *Lost everything*. When he said that, she saw orange groves and automobiles and big white houses falling sadly through the sky. "May I see you home?" he asked, but she went home on the streetcar, with her girlfriends from the telephone company, Vi and Veronica. "May ah see you-all home?" they teased her, in their rough, jokey imitations of a Southern accent. On Monday, when she got off work, he was waiting for her under the arch, hunched against the wind with newspapers stuffed in his vest, holding a rose.

He gave her the rose. He gave her what she'd imagined—she

was waltzing into seventh heaven in the arms of a blue-eyed stranger from the South, where they had plantations and moss in the trees. "You have the eyes of a banished princess," he told her. This was news to her. She'd never heard of *banished*. "Or of a princess locked in a tower." It was the first time she ever reminded anybody except herself and Josie of any kind of princess.

Florida boy. *Mout' fulla mush*, her brothers said when they met him. They didn't want him around, they didn't trust him, they didn't want him for her. Her brothers were the ones who sniffed around and found out he was divorced. He forgot to tell her that. But it was too late by then—she'd gotten used to her dream coming true, she couldn't give it up. She'd never find another one like him. So she forgave him, even though it meant she had to leave the Church and her beloved statues of the Virgin and St. Theresa and St. Catherine and Christ himself, dying on the cross, his beautiful white shoulders lifted, his arms stretched out with their long muscles and blue veins. She had prayed to God, and Gil was what God sent, so she figured it was all right with Him. His scarred heart reminded her a little of Christ's sacred wounded heart. And the way his head sometimes fell to one side when he was thinking, like Christ's in His crown of thorns.

Her mother didn't speak much English. When Rosa took Gilbert home and showed them all her wedding ring, her mother held her hands over her heart, then crossed herself and wept. Rosa remembered her mother's square, foreign figure, and the mahogany veneer credenza behind her, where the candles burned in their red cups before the picture of the Virgin. The wedding ring on her mother's finger flashed in the candlelight when she crossed herself. *You should talk*, Rosa had thought, remembering the way her mother had posed for her picture at Uncle Rudy's in Michigan, in the doorway of the barn, looking into the distance with dreamy eyes, arms full of flowers. Forty-five years old, seven children, was too late for dreamy looks. Those hands like big white turnips hanging in the folds of her long silk skirt when she got married again finally to a man fifteen years younger than herself that she brought in for Emma, and Emma wouldn't look at. *You should cross yourself for your own husband, and where is he tonight?* Rosa had thought meanly when her mother cried about Gilbert.

Rosa was falling asleep in the green hospital chair. She got up to go home. She thought maybe she should lean over and kiss Gilbert, but in the end she just walked out the door and down the empty hall, feeling light, as though she'd forgotten her purse, but there it was on her arm.

Nearly dawn when she got out to the deserted parking lot. She drove slowly, following the exit signs, and ended up at the door to the emergency room. She went back around, paying attention, but then she was at the emergency door again. Around and around, following the signs, doing what they said. She didn't get panicky, she wasn't surprised when she would come out once more at the side of the hospital. She just started through the turns again, a little faster. She couldn't see what she was doing wrong. She couldn't see what else to do. Finally, a young man in a uniform came out of the building and waved her down.

"I'm trying to get out," she told him, her heart pounding. "I don't know what I'm doing wrong."

He thought she was drunk, she knew. She held onto the steering wheel. He bent to look in the window at her, then shifted his weight and said, "Just go up to the end of the lane there and turn left, ma'am."

"Thank you. I'm"—she knocked her knuckles against her forehead—"confused. My husband's in the hospital." She was talking too loud. She could tell by the way his eyes blinked and got polite.

The man went through the instructions again. Even so, she

overshot the turn and bucked the car getting it into reverse. What he must think!

Going around and around like that. She was confused. She knew it. *Poor Rosa.* She had heard Gil tell the kids on the telephone, "Your mother's gotten so forgetful. She doesn't seem to take in what's said. She says the same thing over and over. I'm worried about her." She might be confused, but she knew what *that* meant—poor Gilbert, stuck for life, worry about *him*. Maybe they ought to worry—"Are you trying to kill him?" That's what Dr. Jordan had said.

At home she lay awake watching the darkness come away from the wall, the chairs. The mirror had light in it.

○

When she was five or six, she stole a ride on a bread wagon—they all did it, in her neighborhood. But that time, the wagon didn't stop at Mr. Vronka's store, where it usually did. It kept right on moving, turning corners, until she gave up hope. She hung on for dear life as it carried her away from her neighborhood. She didn't dare jump off. When it finally stopped, she was in a part of town she'd never seen. She stood on the curb, crying, while the bread man yelled at her. She didn't understand that she was lost and could be taken back where she came from. She thought just the opposite—that where she came from was lost, the way you might lose a ball or a doll, forever. The bread man took her to the police station. Her knees shook—she thought they would lock her in jail for stealing the ride, but they took her home. At home, they hadn't missed her yet.

But that night, her mother let her sleep in the bed with her. She wound up the silver music box, the one that Rosa's father had brought from the Old Country when he came to marry Rosa's mother. She sat down on the edge of the bed with the music box in her lap, smoothing

Rosa's hair while it played the old song. When it ran down, her mother wound it up again and sat listening to it with her, over and over, singing the words now and then, until Rosa fell asleep.

The fever scarred my heart, Rosa.

She and Gil got married. How long after that, five years? Nancy just an infant, Tommy maybe two. The pretty bungalow off Ogden Avenue, with the nice backyard and the kitchen they had painted yellow, with the breakfast set from Carl and Shirley. *A sweet little nest.*

She would bundle the children up and put them both in the buggy and take them to meet the streetcar when Gil came home. When the children were in bed, she and Gil would smoke a cigarette or dance to the music on the radio. Or, as on this night, they would sit at the table till all hours, drinking coffee, while Gil told her stories. How Guy Lombardo had come into the furniture department of Marshall Field, where Gil was working by then, to buy a studio couch, and complimented Gil for being such a knowledgeable salesman. Or how Gil had told someone off, in no uncertain terms.

His soft Southern voice, his handsome face with its boyish features, his white teeth and quick, blue eyes. He was different from the people around her, her rough, sturdy brothers—playful, light on his feet, full of nonsense. He could talk to anybody, he had graduated college. He knew how to express himself, he used beautiful English. She was trying to improve her grammar, to say "this" instead of "dis." To improve her manners, her way of eating. He took her to Florida to meet his family. They were all thin and lived in houses with big cool rooms and screened porches, and the women all wore light-colored plaid dresses. They sat under the trees and fanned themselves and drank iced tea with slices of orange in it. They sat mending, smiling at their needles while Gil talked to them. "Well, I swan," they would say, cooing like a bunch of pigeons.

His life was exciting to her, full of adventures and strange doings. "The craziest thing happened today," he said, this time, tinkling his spoon against the side of his coffee cup. And so she opened out a newspaper on the table and started paring apples while he told his story.

It was about walking down Michigan Avenue during his lunch hour and hearing someone calling, "Gil! Gil Cannon!" He turned around and *who* should come running up to him but his old skipper from the banana boat! He threw his arms around Gil and said—she remembered the exact words to this day—"What in tarnation are you doing in *this* burg?" So they went and had a cup of coffee together, and then, *out of the blue*, the skipper had invited him to join his crew, as second mate.

And offered him three times what he was earning at Marshall Field!

Dumb her, she sat there, still nodding, the smile still pasted across her face, an apple in her hand, half pared, as he told her, in a chipper voice, that the skipper's boat was leaving Tampa, destination Rio, at the end of that very month, November.

He took a drink of coffee, in a pleased way, and put the cup back down. Then, for a minute he said nothing, as though he had just caught on to the meaning of what he was saying, needed a little time to put a new light in his eyes. "I've thought it over, Rosa. I don't see how in the world I can turn down an offer like that. Do you?"

She looked at the apple parings, trying to think if there was any answer she could give to that question. Finally she got up her courage and asked, "What about your heart?"

"My job will be mostly paperwork." Then he added, to put her in her place, "Skipper knows about my heart condition better than anyone, of course. When I had malaria, he couldn't have worried about me more if I'd been his own son." He looked down at his cup and went on, in a nice humble voice, "In fact, he told me this afternoon that he had always thought of me as the son he never had." He put his hand on the table, admiring his fingernails, it looked like. "We'll have a lot more money to live on than we have now. It's just that I'll only be here between trips." She got up, without a plan. How long it took to get from Tampa to Brazil and back again was something she didn't know. She went to the sink, turned on the hot water. "Every four, five months, I suppose," he said, in back of her. "For a couple of weeks. Then I'll have to turn right around and do it all again." He wasn't even trying to sound sad. He sounded thrilled. Like they should both be thrilled, for the wonderful new life he was going to have. She felt her face breaking into pieces, just like a plate. She stood running hot water over her hands, holding her shoulders rigid so that they wouldn't shake, thinking of her life with him that he didn't want.

Oh, she won. Her big victory, it wasn't that hard. She forgot how.

No, she remembered. Down on her knees, that's how. She had thought that any minute he would turn, button his coat, and walk out the door. "The chance," he was saying, "the chance of a lifetime. I've got to take it." *No* was all she thought, *no* all through her, making her that heavy, that she fell on her knees, *no* and *no* and *no* coming out of her, big ugly sobs, tears running down her face, down her dress. *Don't leave, don't go, what would I do, two small babies, don't,* and his face bent toward her then, scared, his blue eyes wide open. Gathering her up into his arms. She won, oh yes. "Don't, Rosa," he pleaded, his own eyes full of tears. "Don't. That's enough. I'm not going. Forgive me, dear." Later he said, "I'll call Skipper at his hotel, first thing tomorrow, and tell him it's out of the question. It was just such a surprise—it swept me off my feet."

"Although," he said, shaking his head, his eyes narrowed as

though they were looking across the sea to Brazil, "although that job would have been the making of me."

"You won't be sorry," she promised him.

He never mentioned the banana boat again after that night. She had loved him for that, for not holding it against her, all he might have done if she hadn't held him back.

Then, five years later, Gilbert had three heart attacks in a row, and they moved back to his hometown in Florida, on the doctor's advice. They stayed the first few months with his brother Branham and Branham's wife, Jo, until Gilbert found work and got on his feet.

She and Jo, knitting socks for the prisoners of war out of khaki yarn from the Red Cross, making meat loaves with plenty of stale bread in them, walking Ton, the English bull that Rosa taught to sing the scale. Folding sheets at the clothesline. "When Gilbert had malaria in Brazil," Rosa mentioned.

"I beg your pardon?"

"When he was on the banana boat."

Jo came ducking through the laundry, laughing. "Rosa! The banana boat!" she said in her Southern, amazed voice. She must have seen the look on Rosa's face; anyway, she stopped laughing. "Oh my dear," she said, putting her arms around her, then stepped back, as if she'd thought it over and made a decision, and snapped down the words the way she snapped down her discards in gin rummy: "Gilbert was never on any banana boat." She thought about it and then added, "He never had malaria, either." She started walking Rosa to the house, holding her hand. "Something was wrong with his heart when he was a child," she explained. "They thought they were going to lose him, don't you know. He had to spend a lot of time in bed, poor little fellow, and so he read a lot. I think that's why he's always had such an active imagination. I've never held it against him, myself." Rosa didn't tell Jo about the night she had begged him to stay, down on her knees. She wondered if Jo would have held *that* against him.

○

The curtains in the bedroom blew out now in the light dawn breeze. She thought, *They'll be blowing out like that on the day I die. I'll be right here, in this bed.*

First he told her that he'd gotten malaria in a jungle in Brazil, and she married him. Then he said he was leaving her and going back there, and she begged him on her knees not to go. And later, when she found out it was all a lie, a terrible lie—what had she done then?

She'd told Virginia she was going to take a little nap and climbed the stairs to the hot second story, where they slept. She'd gotten the bottle of scotch out of the bureau drawer, taken two aspirins and washed them down with a slug from the bottle, and then lain down across the bed, on her back, with her hands behind her head. She'd felt nothing, only the hot sun through the yellow shade and the gray thick pain that rose up into her head and throbbed there. The heat and the liquor together made her sick. She threw up, at last, then washed her face and hands and brushed her teeth, never looking in the mirror. She went back downstairs, took the electric fan onto the back porch, and ironed clothes all afternoon, headache or no headache, every last handkerchief and pillowcase, folded each one, thumped the iron back down on it to crease it into a neat square. *Least said soonest mended,* she told herself. When Gilbert came home from work that night, she asked him if they could go to the movies after dinner, and they did.

She let him off easy.

Years later, the doctors at Johns Hopkins found out that Gilbert had been born with a hole in his heart. Even then, when they walked out of the doctor's office together, she didn't bring up the malaria, the banana boat. A closed subject.

And then came the time when he started having to run over to Lakeland two or three times a week to talk to his accountant, John Soto. Back at dinnertime, whistling.

The mockingbird was sitting in the golden rain tree now, pulling every trick out of his bag. She thought she might as well get up. The light came over the wet grass. The red flowers on the hibiscus bushes opened here and there where the sun touched them.

She'd barely heard of Florida until she was twenty-four.

She sat in the slender cane bedroom chair, pulling on her pantyhose. Her thick shadow rippled on the pale blue rug. Everything in this house was light—rattan, thin antiques from Gilbert's people, rockers of pine and oak, spindle beds, silver and glass that caught the light. A dream come true.

No, just a dream sometimes, when she first woke up. An unfamiliar house. Light, not dark. Light, not heavy. Everything here was light, blowing away, words flew around her head, they were nothing, gnats. Her own mind had blown away, too. Going around and around the parking lot like that. It was a shame.

They'd had good times, sometimes, anyway. The bad with the good. *Three wonderful children*; where were they? Not here. They had flitted through these rooms on their way to their strange lives—Tom, divorced, in an old log cabin in Colorado, with an outhouse and only a woodstove for heat; Nancy, also divorced, no children, by herself on a houseboat on the Ohio River that any tramp could break into and rape her; Stephen, unmarried yet, at thirty-four, down in West Palm Beach, running three times a week to that dinky church where he led the singing, no piano allowed. Stephen came to visit once a month, to talk to her about Jesus. "Don't you want eternal life, Mom?" "No," she told him. "I wouldn't want the trouble. I just want to rest." "That's what eternal life *is*, Mom, rest and joy." Stephen didn't know when to shut up anymore. "Rest in the bosom of Abraham." Who taught him that kind of talk? She could imagine heaven with Mary in it, all the saints, Christ with his halo and stigmata, music from a big organ and a thousand voices singing out over the golden altar. But that was gone, and Stephen's heaven, with no piano, wasn't for her. "I just want to rest in the ground, Stephen. I just want to forget about it."

She couldn't imagine anything heavier than having to be Rosa, Rosa, Rosa, through all eternity.

None of her children had found true love. Once she had said this to Tom, tears in her eyes, and he had laughed and said, "*God*, you're full of sentimental drivel, Mom."

She put on her dark blue pants, her nice dark blue and crimson T-shirt. She slipped her dendrite from Brazil around her neck on its silver chain. She hated her arms, covered with dark hair, her short bowed legs, her crooked toes from wearing shoes that were too small when she was a kid. They'd still be crooked when she was dead. Unless she was cremated. That's what Gil wanted. He wanted his ashes to be scattered over the Gulf of Mexico. Her lids drooped over her brown eyes. The eyes of a princess locked in a tower, ha.

She leaned into the mirror, smoothed on her lipstick with her little finger the way she had done ever since she was a young girl, a 1920's girl. She'd had her life; it stretched back. "Face it, Nancy, your mother's an old woman," she had said on the telephone the other day. "Nobody lasts forever, kid." Gilbert would go first, though. Not this time, but another.

Faraway places with strange-sounding names. She remembered his face, so intelligent, so happy, as he bent to the road map, marking the roads they would take to get to Devil's Lake, in Michigan, in the car her brother-in-law John Gianelli let them borrow. Later, with the kids hanging over his shoulder, he was always sitting at the dining room table, a map spread out in the lamplight, tracing the road they were going to take to get somewhere, the Grand Canyon, Niagara Falls, telling them what they'd see along the way and where they were going to stop.

He should have had a clean life on the high seas.

She should have had a kind, loving, quiet husband who didn't lie all the time. And who didn't cheat on her. A sickly child in bed reading adventure books. Why didn't he go then? When he grew up? He could have gotten a job on a boat, couldn't he? Maybe, because of his heart, they wouldn't hire him, or maybe he didn't think he was strong enough. So he lived an adventurous life in his mind, made up stories, and turned into a talker. A blowhard, a liar. Or maybe he was too lazy. Maybe all he ever really wanted was to talk about it, not do it.

"Well, I'm staying here," she had told him yesterday. "That's final." Which was when he went out to edge the lawn.

A nice cup of coffee and a roll was what she wanted for her breakfast. A good fresh sweet roll, like what they ate in Chicago when she was a kid, from her Aunt Jewel's bakery, prunes tucked inside and flakes of coconut and nice slivered almonds on top. You couldn't get that in Florida.

What would have happened if she'd been another kind of woman, able to say, with no anger, no fear, "You're right. The chance of a lifetime, go and make three times as much as at Marshall Field, and when you come back, we'll paint the town. But let's just get it fixed up so those checks come through, honey." Where would he have gone, no skipper, no banana boat? If she had called his bluff, would he have stayed, made a big production out of deciding to stay? Or walked out the door forever?

If he'd walked out the door, she wouldn't have seen him again, she was pretty sure. And then what would have happened to her?

She was standing now in front of the open refrigerator, with no idea why, the jar of instant coffee in her hand. She got out the milk and closed the door, put some corn flakes in a bowl.

They'd seen the world, anyway. They'd been to Majorca, Spain, Portugal, Mexico, England, Hawaii—she couldn't remember. The Islands. To Brazil. He couldn't get enough of Brazil. She'd lost track of how many times they went there, after his business in Florida started bringing in money.

Once, in Brazil, they took a tram up a mountain to see that famous statue of Christ. On the way down, the power went out and all the passengers had to get off and walk back to the station in the pitch dark. Rosa fell into an open manhole and hurt herself, and had to walk, Gilbert and a Brazilian man who didn't speak English half-carrying her, all the rest of the way down the mountain into the station. Finally, she had fainted from the pain. She'd thought she was dying then. It turned out she'd cracked two ribs. They took her to the hospital, and then from the hospital to the hotel, in an ambulance. Gilbert was wonderful that time, staying close beside her, bringing her meals in bed, going to get the prescriptions filled. She'd gotten up as soon as she could walk without fainting and gone with him everywhere again, her chest tightly bandaged. She didn't want to ruin his trip. She felt glad that he was so proud of her. "This gal here," he told the children, when they got back home, "is the bravest mortal God ever made."

She was brave about some things.

Her faraway place had always been a man. He'd spent his childhood reading books about adventure; she'd spent hers wrapped up in organdy curtains, making up something that would happen. She couldn't remember what, exactly. Some big romance. To be waltzed away from herself—or was it into herself?—in the arms of a man. In the arms of the man of her dreams. That was what they all wanted, the girls, when she was young.

All she wanted now was just what she had, and to keep it.

She couldn't remember the names of all the places they'd been. He came back and showed his slides to the Kiwanis Club, told about his trips to anyone who happened to drop by. *The bluest water I have ever seen; the finest fish I ever put in my mouth, bar none.* People seemed to like to hear. The excited voice, wanting nothing but to go on and on, and be listened to with respect. He said what he had to say, to get attention. That they'd been invited to a party for Sophia Loren, when they'd really only overheard somebody talking about it in the bar. "Oh?" she would say, rolling her eyes at whoever else was in the room, to warn them. "*I* don't remember that." Only now she didn't even remember the things that really happened, so nobody took her warning.

Her blood had heaviness in it. It sank into silence. The more he talked, the further she sank down into the thing like a well, alone down there, wanting less and less. Words were only the blizzard that flew around her head. She paid more attention to the mockingbird.

Stupid woman, Gil had said once, in a loud voice, right out on the street. Once, when he was mad at her. She wasn't stupid. She had earned her living from when she was fourteen until she was six months gone with Tommy. And before she went to work, eleven, twelve, she was already taking care of a house and two little boys. She had the best handwriting in school. Once, when the regular girl was absent, the nuns asked her to play the piano for the children to march into their classes in the morning. And she'd never had a lesson, just picked it up by ear.

○

From outside the door of his room, she saw him sitting up, spooning oatmeal into his mouth. He was smiling his twinkling devilish Ike grin at the nurse, a short, older woman, like herself. The nurse smiled at her, going out of the room, and whispered, "He's much better."

When he caught sight of Rosa, he pressed his lips together and held out his hand—they should celebrate, he was still alive.

"You look pretty good, for an old man," she said in a jolly voice.

His face shaded over with a sharp, displeased look. He'd had a close call, she shouldn't forget.

"Did you get some sleep?"

"For a few hours. They woke me up to do some tests." He picked up his glass of orange juice. "Dr. Jordan's not completely satisfied with my condition."

"Oh."

He looked down into his glass, swirling the orange juice like it was a scotch on the rocks. He was waiting for her; he wanted her to show how worried she was. She felt tired, tired. Fooling with this crazy man all her life. She put her face down into the overnight case she had packed, started taking out his new pajamas, his clean underwear. She felt suddenly clammy, sick. She sat down in the chair in the corner, pressed her cold fingers into her eyes. Begging him like that, down on her knees, not to leave her.

"Rosa, are you all right?" She was scaring *him* now. She couldn't help it. She couldn't think about it.

"Rosa?" His voice was full of fright. Real fright, not made up. He cared about her. He wanted to take care of her, he *had* taken care of her, all these years, but she couldn't think about it. She felt sick, sick, for her life. She pressed her cold fingers up against the bony ridges where her forehead began, trying to remember herself in the old days, before she started turning into this other one, this dull, heavy, confused one. A nice, smart young woman, a pretty, soft young woman, in a crimson dress, wanting romance, love, marriage, children, what they all wanted, back then. *I'll be loving you, always. With a love that's true, always.*

What had she meant, what had any of them meant? They hadn't known—something wonderful, that was all. Something real, of their own.

Down on her knees, to keep what she had, to keep what she had from walking out the door on her, those big sobs coming out of her. Maybe that was part of what the songs had taught her, that pain. The blues. Heartbreak. But later, ironing those clothes all afternoon, that wasn't the blues anymore. There was no song about the sick heavy headache, about waiting for him to come home from work so that she could begin to pretend not to know what she knew. She'd pretended all these years.

Fear and fear and fear making a liar out of *her*, too. There would never be an end to it now. It was too late to untangle her life from his. Like trying to untangle the roots of two plants growing a long time in the same pot. In five years they'd both be dead. No use.

But it wasn't that. *Never too late*, she heard the stern words—even now, at the end, it was fear. Even now, not to lose.

But what if he made her leave her house? What then?

It wouldn't happen. She wasn't going to leave, and he wouldn't leave without her. She knew it. She'd seen that sharp look of fear flash out of his eyes when she said, "Go then."

He wouldn't have left that other time, either, but she hadn't known it, then. Too dumb. He had no place to go. He'd just wanted the *idea* of it, poor man: that something like that could happen to some poor so-and-so walking through the Loop in the icy wind, on his lonely lunch hour from selling furniture, and then home to the four-room bungalow off Ogden. It wasn't that he hated their life together. He just got started and couldn't stop. And there was Rosa, down on her knees, saying, "Don't go! Don't leave us!" What a chump. Guy Lombardo had never come into the furniture department, either.

She took her hands away from her eyes, rubbed them together, hard. "You're pale!" he cried. "I'm going to ring for the nurse."

"No, I'm okay now. I just got woozy for a minute."

He looked at her still. He didn't know what to do; he put his hand on her forehead. Her head ached, but the wave of nausea had passed. She took a deep breath; she got a tissue and dried her face. "Hey," she said, "that's a cute outfit, mister. Hubba hubba. Let's see what it looks like from the back."

He told everybody all day long, "Rosa has simply worried herself *sick*."

"Look," she said. "I brought the paper for you. And a deck of cards." There was nothing wrong with him. She wasn't going to act sympathetic.

"Hot diggity dog," he said.

Neighbors, friends, poker cronies dropped in through the day. He was on top of the world, bright, jokey. The center of attention. He forgot about the doctor not being satisfied with his condition. He turned *not* being at death's door into a way to get attention. In between visits, they played gin rummy. He got mad at her for forgetting what she'd discarded. "Thank you very much," he'd say, picking up the queen of spades. "I just *took* the jack."

"Oh so what. I'll still win."

Dr. Jordan showed up in the afternoon and said he could go home the next morning. Gilbert turned to her, pretending to be overjoyed instead of disappointed. "Rosa," he said, for Dr. Jordan's benefit. "I want you to be here at eight-thirty sharp. Really and truly," he told Dr. Jordan, "I don't know when in my life I've been so anxious to be home."

"You know what?" he asked, later. She shook her head, staring at the bed rail. She couldn't look at him. "Even that damned old yard will look pretty good to me."

She nodded. "I'll get everything ready for you," she said, from a little distance, feeling formal.

○

There were many other cars leaving the parking lot that night; she only had to follow the leader.

She wished she hadn't begged that time, but it was over now. It was like wishing she had been a different person.

She didn't have any pictures of herself as a child, but later on, after work sometimes, she would pose in the photo booth at the dime store, in her shingled haircut with the finger waves set in, or her plaid wool dress with the fancy white collar. Nobody took her picture so she took her own, smiling in her new velvet beret at some imaginary sweetheart. A thin girl with big sad brown eyes. Not meant to live alone. Gilbert had found these little snapshots, the size of postage stamps, and pasted them all on one page of the photograph album he started when they got married. At the bottom of the page he wrote, "Ten Good Reasons for Coming to Chicago."

She'd gotten what she prayed for. They'd had their long life together, three wonderful children. They'd had good times together, sometimes. He'd cheated on her, but he came back and begged her to forgive him. She took him back.

But she never forgave him. Couldn't forgive and couldn't let go, either. Took him back, but kept up her savings account, just in case.

He wouldn't leave. They'd be together for the rest of their lives. In the empty house, she made herself a stiff bourbon and water and drank it at the kitchen sink, then poured herself another little jigger, so she would sleep this time, and took it into the bedroom. She sat back against the pillows, sipping it. Maybe it could be funny now, though it hadn't been funny at the time. A banana boat. You really had to laugh. Poor lying Gilbert, poor dumb scared Rosa, so long ago. Now they were old and still together, hooray—one with no mind, the other crazy.

Such are the vicissitudes, she thought, but in her chest was something tight, like a fist, a tight, angry sorrow for her life, almost done with now.

What if she hadn't begged that time? What if he'd left? What kind of life would she have had? She'd never even tried to imagine it. Not an easy one, maybe even a sad one. It wasn't like nowadays, with child support—back then, the man could just take a powder. No trips, no college for the kids, maybe not even enough to eat. Back to work at the telephone company. No father for them, no husband for her. No baby Stephen coming along to make her glad as her hair turned gray.

But they would have survived, she guessed, the three of them. Tom and Nancy and her, Rosa Vronka. She hadn't even considered it. "No," was all she had considered.

"It all seems like a dream," she'd say, walking through the strange streets of Brazil. But she'd gotten something out of it, too. They had seen those falls down there, they'd gone down that river, and one night, that time she cracked her ribs, she'd heard piano music playing over a loudspeaker from the movie house across from the hotel. A simple little song, but it halted and turned in a sweet, surprising way. The record played over and over. She didn't get tired of it. Gilbert, after a long day of staying by her bed, had gone down to the hotel bar. "I think I'll see if I can scare up somebody to shoot the breeze with," he'd said. She sat by herself, the wide bandage wound tightly around her rib cage. In the dark, at the open window, one floor above the square, she had sat watching the people who lived in the town strolling by. Sometimes a voice would float up to her. A woman with brown hair in a braid around her head came along the street with some loaves of bread in a basket. *That could be me*, she'd thought, and suddenly the life of that woman filled her up: she walked through the crowd with long strides, her flowered skirt swinging against her legs. She went in a door. Rosa imagined her putting the bread on a table, turning and striking a match to light the stove.

Rosa had sat at that window for a long time, her hands on the wide sill, enjoying herself. The bells of the old church rang out eleven times, but still small children ran around. A man with a short white pony was giving rides around the square. He had a red scarf tied around his neck, and the pony had one, too, to match. Rosa still remembered one child, a girl, four or five years old, in a yellow dress and bright blue tights. As the man lifted her down from the pony, he swung her around and around; her little blue legs flew out, she screamed a high, excited scream.

Rosa had sat there at the window until she heard Gilbert's key in the lock. Then she pulled the curtains together and lay down on the bed with her eyes closed. She didn't want to hear what had happened in the bar. She didn't want to tell him about the little girl—it would just turn into one of his stories. She lay beside him with her eyes closed, listening to the song playing over and over. She lay still and breathed in and out.

Ten, fifteen years ago, that was. That girl would be a young woman by now.

The bourbon had made Rosa lightheaded. Her body seemed to float upward, away from her bones, to turn as the room was turning, in sliding circles. She switched off the lamp and laid her head back carefully on the pillow. No breath in this room now but her own. She stared for a minute into the empty sliding darkness, then closed her eyes against it. Something still turned like a slow Ferris wheel behind her eyes. It made her feel sick. To take her mind off it, she remembered—just in her head, not out loud—that sweet melody from the movie house. The white pony. The little girl in blue stockings, swinging out, swinging out, screaming for joy.

TODO EL MUNDO

A shadow moved through the opening. At the edge of her vision, as she came awake, the bathroom door pulled to and noiselessly closed. She lay frozen in her bed, her heart racing, staring through two rooms at the closed white door of the bathroom. Something behind it now, waiting her out.

Surely she had closed the door herself, before she went to bed.

But she had seen it *closing*.

What would she do now?

She thought of something. She slid quickly out of bed, ran barefoot across the tiles, slapped the screen door shut behind her, to let the one behind the door know she was no longer in the house. Now what would *he* do? She had him trapped!

She sat rigidly, ready for flight, in a canvas chair on her terrace, from which she could watch the closed door. If the door began to open, she could scream. She wasn't alone here. The house was divided into two apartments. She had the lower one. If she screamed, her neighbors upstairs would hear her.

She sat on the edge of the chair, never taking her eyes off the door, for—she didn't know how long. Her plan was to sit out here until Felipe, the gardener, showed up at seven. Then they could open the door together.

Gradually, Leila became aware of the sweet heavy tropical darkness that enclosed her, smelling of jasmine and wet green leaves, gardenias and sea. The wind got up. The soft island air played over her skin. Finally she allowed herself to lean back in the chair and yawn. She said to herself: *And just what would this person have in mind, shutting himself up in your bathroom?* When she was able to pose this question, she was able to walk inside and pull open the bathroom door to confront—nothing.

Oh, it was always nothing. And the roosters crowing down in the barrios. Nothing, and beyond the hills, beyond the spill of the city, the gleam of the sea in the distance, gathering light just before there was light to gather, the sounds of traffic beginning to rise from the highway, and then the man who shouted "*Chinas y naranjas!*" along her road, the sky softening and the sun rising out of the ocean, the gentle morning rain falling on the shining leaves.

For she lived in paradise.

She'd been on her own for six or seven years now, sometimes in big dangerous cities, taking all sorts of chances. She'd never been frightened before. She'd never thought of herself as a nervous person. But she had bad dreams, here in paradise.

What woke her, what terrified her, always turned out to be nothing. Followed by another beautiful day.

○

The next time Leila saw the door closing, a week or so later, she woke herself screaming, "Help! Help! There's someone in here!" Hank Plant, her neighbor, was down the stairs almost before she'd gotten the light on; she unlocked her bedroom door, opening onto the terrace, to let him in. "Ain't nobody going to get *you*, Leila," he said, his pistol held upward by his ear, his wrist bent backward. Leila, aghast at what she'd set in motion, already knowing there was no one in any of her rooms, could hardly keep from doubling over with laughter at the sight of Hank, who looked like Robert Mitchum a little past his prime, going through her house in his T-shirt and boxer shorts, opening her closet door, looking under her bed. But she was also shaking, hard, standing on her terrace now, in her blue nightgown, until Cass, Hank's wife, who had followed him down the stairs, put her arm around Leila and led her to the chairs by the round white patio table. They sat, huddled together, watching Hank pressed back against the wall, stretching an arm to swing open the bathroom door, the revolver cocked high in the other hand, in the age-old Robert Mitchum way.

When they were all satisfied that no one was there, Cass, in her fresh pink-and-white seersucker robe, ran upstairs to get a bottle of brandy and a bathrobe for Hank. Leila went inside and put on her own big terrycloth bathrobe, and brought out three glasses. They sat around the table in the dark together, the three of them, drinking, in a holiday mood, relieved and exhilarated, as if no one had to go to work in the morning. Then, shocking herself, Leila lowered her head onto her folded arms and started to cry. She felt stupid and neurotic. But she couldn't stop.

And the Plants were wonderfully kind. "Don't you ever worry about waking us up, if you think you hear something," Cass said, in a sweet, motherly voice, rubbing her back.

"Or if you're just scared. You come right on upstairs," Hank added. "We'd do anything in the world for you, honey."

"It's the full moon, I guess," Leila apologized.

○

She tried to remember to lock all the doors of her apartment at night—there were four, each room opening onto the wide terrace. But sometimes when she woke thinking someone was in the house, she believed that she had overlooked one of them. And oddly, given her fear, it turned out, sometimes, that she had.

She felt vulnerable here, on this island, for the first time in her life. Noticeable—noticed. Set apart by her tall, unmistakably Anglo-Saxon looks, her awkwardness with Spanish. Her singleness.

But she was happy enough, in the daylight. Felipe, a smiling, solid old man with a pipe, often left gardenias on the terrace table for her in the mornings, mangoes, papayas. When it rained, Felipe, water running down his wide smiling face, told her, "*Sin agua, no hay vida.*" Without water, there is no life.

In the daylight, Leila prepared her classes, dressed for work, drove down the hill, and then along the highway to the university, where she taught English as a second language. Later, she changed into her shorts and ran on the beach, or came home and played her blues albums.

Sometimes, in the evenings, she had dinner with the Plants, who were from Alabama, and in their mid-forties. Hank Plant worked for an architectural firm as a civil engineer. Cass read and cooked, a Southern belle adrift, it seemed to Leila, in a foreign world, where her old pearl earrings, her complex hors d'oeuvres, her soft musical voice and twelve place settings of ornate sterling flatware simply did not convey the message she had relied upon them to convey all her life.

"Not what I'm used to," Cass murmured to Leila, who was the nearest thing in a thousand miles to what she was used to—at least Leila could be depended upon to *get* the message, even if she didn't believe a word of it, herself. She'd been raised in the South, too—some twenty years after Cass, it was true, but things didn't change fast, where she came from. Leila had traveled a long way from home, gone to a lot of trouble, to get away from what she was used to. From her own set of sterling.

She often accepted Cass and Hank's invitations to dinner only because she couldn't see how not to. She lived right downstairs from them. They could see she had no other plans, though sometimes she said she had too much work, or had already eaten, or was asleep on her feet. Besides, Cass was a good cook, and it was easy, after a day of struggling to make herself understood by her students, to take the path of least resistance.

She'd gotten into the habit of drinking too much since she came to the island. Liquor was everywhere—it was cheap and went down easy, in the tropical frame of mind she'd fallen into. No one she knew—except her students' parents—had fewer than two cocktails before dinner. Then wine, glass after glass, as if it were water, through dinner, and afterward, with coffee, a tray of liqueurs to choose among. The Plants were frequently drunk. Cass, while they were in the cocktail-hour phase, sat in her pretty plum-colored shorts, her toenails painted to match, her bare feet tucked under her demurely, a cigarette dangling between her thin fingers as she raised a glass of rum-something in a ladylike way to her lips, her gold bracelets falling up her arm. Cass looked like an ex-homecoming queen, small, pert, with beautiful shiny tanned legs and a sweetly provocative, slightly bucktoothed profile, bright brown eyes. Hank, on the other hand, was tall, physically and socially expansive, flirtatious, a little dissolute, droopy-eyed. His lax, kind body still suggested the handsome, lean young man he must have been. Together, they were the kind of couple Cass liked to describe as "vair attraictive."

During this twilit hour, Cass and Hank seemed happy together, as happy as anyone, listening courteously to what the other was saying, Hank leaning forward to light Cass's cigarettes. Then there was the ceremony of the elegant, lavish dinner, which was always served on the Plants' roofed front porch, overlooking the sunset on one side, the lighted city with its mini-skyline and the ocean on the other. Toward the end of dinner (Hank always vigilant to the empty wineglasses), the first slight disagreement would have been engaged, the first irritation expressed. If it was possible, Leila slipped down the stairs when the real argument, the sharp invective, flared, with dessert. Occasionally, in the middle of the night, she heard their voices flung out over the hillside of flowers and palm trees, Hank's baffled and bellowing, or heavily laying down the law, Cass's hanging onto its careful Southern diphthongs, only ratcheted up a notch into shrill, prim hysteria, ringing up and down the scale of dissatisfaction, disappointment, boredom. Leila didn't hear the words, just the tone, as she closed her eyes and folded the pillow around her ears.

She'd been on the island for two years, but in this apartment for only the past ten months. When she'd found it, she had barely been able to believe her luck—each room overlooking the lush, neglected hillside, a sweep of shining leaves. It simply hadn't occurred to her, in her delight, to wonder what it would be like to live so close up against other people, with no anonymity possible, how much she would be forced to know of the Plants' private life, how little she'd be able to protect her own from being known by them. But, she told herself, for the rent she paid here, she'd be living in somebody's garage in town, or sharing a tiny house with two or three roommates, as she had done before she moved here, speaking of being forced to know more than you wanted to about other people's lives.

And the arguments didn't always happen. Often nothing at all happened, and she could forget that she wasn't alone here. Often there was only sweet island silence, wind and *coquís*, the small transparent tree frogs that sang all night. And then the morning rain.

○

Along with English as a second language, Leila also taught a section of English literature to the more bilingual students, in which she tried to explain what was meant by: "And tear our pleasures with rough strife/Through the iron gates of life." She made a tape for them from her albums and brought it to class one day—Etta James, Howlin' Wolf, Robert Johnson—to try to get them to understand. They liked the music, but she was afraid they didn't make the connection. These students were filled with strange hilarity as they made their way, here, near the end of the term, through John Milton. Leila was beginning to suspect that a lot of them came to class stoned.

After two years on the island, she had learned to dread the end of term, because her students brought her presents. They brought all the teachers presents, of course, but the ones they brought Leila seemed so inappropriate she wondered if they weren't sporting her. But she couldn't believe it—they were so eager and proud. They took up collections, they had excited, whispered conferences. They brought her long purple earrings, pink nightgowns. Bath oils, half-slips. *"¡Ay, qué linda!"* she dutifully exclaimed. She was expecting any day to open a box of underpants, along with a card that said, "Thank you our teacher."

Sometimes students invited her to their families' homes for dinner. She went, because she liked her students very much. She also wanted to learn what real life (as opposed to expatriate-island-gringo life) in this place was like. She practiced her Spanish. She answered her students' mamas' questions, it seemed only polite, about her own mama and papa, about her past, her love life—"*¿Tiene novio?*" they always asked. And were worried and surprised, clicking their tongues in sympathy, when she smilingly shook her head and shrugged.

There was no division between the public and the private on this whole island, apparently. That's how she explained her situation to herself. She couldn't think of any way to keep her students from bringing her nightgowns.

It probably served her right. She was here because of a tourist advertisement—curving white beach, blue water, beachcombing couple in the distance, the usual. At the time that she saw it—during a particularly gray cold winter in the Midwest—it had looked like heaven to her, and, on a whim, she had decided to see if they had a university there among all those palm trees. She'd needed a change, after the long haul of graduate school and then the two years of teaching in a small college surrounded by cornfields and academic squabbles. She had wanted to improve her Spanish and look at water and get away from an earnest, boyish chemistry teacher who seemed determined to marry her.

When she learned her application had been accepted, she was elated, went around singing to herself, "Got the sun to tan me, breeze to fan me, and—an occasional man."

But occasional was beginning to look highly optimistic. Almost everyone over the age of eighteen was married. She had landed on an island shimmering with sex, but none for her, unless she wanted to attack teenagers. Or other people's husbands.

The last man she'd been out with, months before, had been a pompous government official who'd spent the evening telling her about his M.B.A. and giving her a rundown on how much everyone in the room was worth. At some point, as if it were his gentlemanly duty, he had clamped his hand over her breast. When she knocked his hand away, he said, "As I thought. Frigid."

Frigid. She almost wished. Because just a friendly shoulder massage, just a hand on her arm, meant personally, had her digging her fingernails into her palms, against meltdown.

She understood that she was in a dangerous situation here.

She knew the presence-behind-the-door had something to do with sexual deprivation. She was embarrassed about it, and didn't mention it to anyone, least of all, of course, to the Plants. But there was no way to hide from them the fact that she was alone a lot of the time.

The Plants thought it was a shame. "What a waste," they said. They wanted to help her. She didn't know how to get them to stop—didn't even know if she wanted them to stop. She'd imagined, when she came to this island, a kind of retreat. But she hadn't ever envisioned for herself two years of total celibacy.

○

About a week after the screaming incident, Cass left for a week's visit with her daughter in Florida. Leila had known this trip was coming and had felt apprehensive about being alone up here on the hill with Hank, and sure enough, on the evening of Cass's departure, he came home from work and knocked on Leila's door on the way upstairs. "Let's go get us some langostino," he said, loosening his tie.

"Oh, I'm sorry, Hank." Thank God she still had on her work clothes. "I've got a meeting. I have to go back to town. I'm just about to leave."

He looked at her, nodding, his blue eyes distant.

"Another time?" she said, to soften the refusal.

"*¿Cómo no?*" he replied.

She could think of a lot of reasons why not, but it was the literal translation—*how* not—that kept her busy for the next several days.

That first night, she went to visit friends in town and stayed gone till ten.

The next evening, he surprised her by coming home early. She had been planning to be gone by the time he returned. When she heard his car coming up the hill, she shut herself up in the bathroom, turning the shower on full blast, just in case. When he knocked, she was singing over the running water. He kept knocking. She kept singing—belting out her meanest version of "I'd Rather Go Blind." When he quit knocking, she turned off the water, hastily pulled on a skirt and T-shirt, collected her purse and her papers to grade, raced out the door to her car, and got away. That's how she thought of it, as getting away. "This is too weird—I'm going to have to move," she said to herself, buckling her seat belt as she careened out onto the highway.

The next morning, as she was talking on her terrace to Felipe, Hank came down the stairs, on his way to work. "Didn't you hear me yesterday?" he asked, with a jowly, sour look she hadn't seen before. "I knocked and yelled. I thought we were going out together."

"Oh, Hank! If we had some kind of definite plan, I didn't know it."

"You were in the shower," he said, slightly mollified. "Singing your head off."

"Well, that explains why I didn't hear you. Did it sound good?"

"It must have sounded good to *you*. Next thing I knew, you were hightailing it down the road."

"Yeah. To my office. It's getting near the end of the term—it's all catching up with me."

"*El Capitán está furioso,*" observed Felipe, smiling like a crazy person, after Hank had left. "Ha ha ha, *muy furioso.*" Felipe didn't quite understand English, though he enjoyed listening, head moving from one person to the other in jolly curiosity.

The next two nights, she had dinner at school and stayed in her office grading essays till late—if Hank understood that she was avoiding him, too bad. And as it happened, on the weekend she had a legitimate plan (she thought she might have made it when she'd found out Cass was going to Florida by herself) to fly with friends to another island for the weekend. When she got home on Sunday evening, Hank was out; Cass would return on Monday, so Leila felt she'd made it.

That night, Hank came home from somewhere, late. He had a woman with him. She heard them staggering up the steps—a burst of laughter, stifled into high drunken giggles. "Shhh."

That night she dreamt of making love to Hank. Or rather, she dreamt he was sitting in a chair, fully clothed, holding her, fully unclothed, in his lap. When she woke she was horrified, and felt she had betrayed both Hank and Cass. She had seemed, in the dream, to have no will at all, to be caught there. And this description seemed unfair. Hank was raunchy, but kind. As for Cass, she had done everything she could think of to help Leila. It was perfectly true what they'd told her: they'd do anything in the world for her.

○

A few weeks after Cass's return, near the end of Leila's second school year on the island, the Plants gave a party, to which Leila of course was invited. The party had been going on for some little while by the time she got there. A man in his early thirties named Billy Vásquez, an architect who worked with Hank, and whom she had met at the Plants' before, nodded at her from the other side of the room. His wife—Leila gathered her name was Van, though nobody introduced them—was a Garbo-shouldered Irish woman, ruddy and taciturn, taller than Billy. She wore a cotton sundress, the skirt falling between her legs, her bare feet propped on the coffee table. Soon enough, as Van smoked and watched, Billy crossed the room, took Leila's hand and led her onto the roofed porch to dance. He looked at her, in a companionable, inquisitive way, without speaking or smiling, as he drew her toward him.

Billy was a good dancer; so was Leila. She had grown accustomed to the subtle pelvic intimations of this particular dance in the years she'd been here, but dancing with Billy introduced some other category of intimation altogether, something not quite so—specific. Very soon, she gave herself over to his expertise, the action mainly in the hips, suggestive but restrained. His body felt exact. He knew how to hold the tension between pliancy and formality in the spine, as if it were a secret of birth which he now shared with her. Others were on the porch, dancing, or standing and talking. She felt that she was being watched with amused interest, and said to herself, reprovingly, *Oh come on*. When the music ended she couldn't meet Billy's eyes, though she felt his black-eyed gaze all but curving under her lowered eyelids.

Soon afterward, it came to light that the party was out of rum. Billy volunteered to drive down to his place to get more. Someone floated the idea that Billy needed company, and this idea gained jokey support. Leila was soon aware that they were all eyeing her, grinning, speculating. "Hey, don't look at *me*," she said, holding up her hands. Now everyone at the party—they were all much drunker than Leila—everyone, including the wife of Billy Vásquez, became insistent, raucous in their insistence, that Leila go with him. Cass and Hank, along with the others, were beating on the tables now, stamping on the floor, chanting, to her confusion and alarm, "Leila goes along! Leila goes along!" Billy pulled her out the door, laughing, his head thrown back. "Don't worry," said Van Vásquez, stretching an arm out languidly for her glass, as if she didn't give a damn. "He doesn't bite. Not that I ever heard tell."

At the bottom of the steps, on her own terrace, he looked at her with a conspirator's smiling glance. Above them, several people leaned over the Plants' balcony ledge, clapping, cheering. Billy gave them a good-humored, dismissive wave, pulling Leila behind him by the other hand. When they rounded the corner, out of sight of the balcony, he turned to her. "Shall we give them their little thrill? Will you ride down the hill with me? Or do you like now to"—he nodded at Leila's front door—"call it an evening?"

This struck her as a gentlemanly, honorable offer. She was moved by the contrast he made to the leering ones upstairs. They looked at each other, heads tilted, through the darkness.

"They're all very—excitable," he added. "I'm sorry for it."

"They're all very drunk."

"Yes," he agreed equably.

"I'm not going back to the party," she said then, making up her mind. "But I'll ride down the hill with you. You live just down in Cupey, don't you?" She didn't want him to feel she mistrusted him, she told herself. "It'll be all right," she heard herself earnestly assuring someone, unclear whether Billy or herself. He was an artist, she'd heard. Perhaps they could be friends, find something to say to each other.

But also, she was forced to admit to herself (being—at least trying to be—an honest woman), she seemed to have entered a new field of gravity. She couldn't pull back.

He smiled then, a sudden, joyful smile, touched her elbow. "Of course it will."

But before they got to the bottom of the hill, he had slid his hand over Leila's shoulder. He carefully parted her hair so that it fell on either side of her neck. "For weeks," he said, in his direct voice, "since

I first saw you, I have wanted to touch this exact place. What do you call it? Nape?" She was speechless, but moved in a way that forbade her, for a moment, from gathering herself and sliding away from him, as his fingers moved lightly, knob by knob, down her spine to the collar of her blouse, and then beneath it a little way. "The exact place where your so-straight spine meets your skull." And his fingers traced upward again to probe the softness there at the juncture, to comb slowly through her parted hair, one side, then the other. She sat up, took a breath, moved away from him. She was surprised to notice that her lips seemed to be buzzing—too much rum, no doubt.

They drove in silence the short distance to his house—a new house in a tract where bulldozers had, within her own memory of the place, cleared away a hillside of beautiful old trees. Now one concrete-block house after another had sprung up, each scraped plot paved with a driveway and a curved concrete patio, a few yards of lawn and perhaps a seedling tree between the patio and the street.

She turned her head to look over her shoulder at the darkened house. She felt tense, and understood that it was half with longing. As though, unless she braced herself, she could be pushed over the edge by a breath. When he turned off the motor, he reached to turn her head toward him. "Won't you come in with me?"

"No."

"I won't harm you. I would like to show you the paintings I have made—forgive me, Leila, don't laugh. If you see them, you'll know I'm not a bad person."

"I don't think you're a bad person, Billy. Just get the rum. I want to go back."

He looked at her gravely. "All right," he said then.

When he returned, he handed her the bottle through the open window. He glanced at her sweetly as he slid behind the wheel, then, without hesitation, took the bottle out of her hands and drew her to him. Her body against his felt as though it had lost its bones, turned into a kind of ocean. "Oh, you need me," he murmured. "You do."

"Did you all have a bet?" she asked, pushing away from him, her eyes stinging now. "What did you bet?"

"You misunderstand me," he told her, sadly. His lips didn't match, she noticed. The upper lip was thin and rather severe, the lower one full, smooth, sensual.

"What about your wife? Does she misunderstand you?"

He looked at her with a reproachful smile. "My wife and I have our arrangements," he said then. "We understand each other perfectly."

"Well, maybe your wife and you ought to arrange something else. Something that doesn't include me. I want to go back. I want you to take me home."

He turned the key. Without another word, he drove her back. It wasn't anger, or even disappointment, coming from him, as she had expected. It was something she hardly knew how to identify, a sort of composed solicitude—concern, not too far removed from the soft clicking sounds her students' mothers made when they heard she didn't have a *novio*. Almost maternal. Almost kind. It reminded her of the dance, restraint in deep alliance with the insistent beat, the hoarse, hard-pressed voice of the singer. She leaned her head back against the seat and rubbed her forehead. At her house, she got out of the car before he'd turned off the motor, went up the path without waiting for him and through her own door, locking it behind her.

She locked all the doors, got in bed with her clothes on, hearing the howls of laughter upstairs as Billy returned to the party without her. "Close, so close," she heard Hank say. She felt panicky, for a moment, surrounded, ganged up on, half expecting them to troop down the stairs and bang pots outside her window, insisting on something else they'd thought of. But then she told herself, *They're just a bunch of drunk, bored jerks, that's all.* And what about Billy Vásquez? *Then you'll know I'm not a bad person, Christ.* She folded the pillow around her ears. *No wonder I have bad dreams*, she told herself.

○

She avoided the Plants for several days, seriously hoped never to speak to them again. Finally, Cass came to the door. "Are you all right, Leila? Are you mad with us?"

"Of course I'm mad with you. What did you think you were doing?"

"Well, if you didn't want to go with him you should have said." Leila glared at Cass but didn't answer, since what Cass said was obviously true. "Oh come on, what did we do? Handcuff you? You wanted to be with him, didn't you? We thought we were—helping. He's awful cute," she said, her voice lilting upward. Then she made her face serious and added, confidentially, "And I know he's rill, rill attracted to you. He told Hank he is."

Though she hated it, this information sent a thrill through Leila. "He's taken, Cass," she said in a cold voice.

"Oh, well now, there's taken and there's *taken*, isn't there." She gave Leila a look, one eyebrow raised sexily.

Leila wondered, fleetingly, if Cass had been to bed with Billy Vásquez, in her heirloom pearl earrings. If Cass knew that her own husband, the minute her plane took off, had been knocking on Leila's door. It came to her with a soft pop of revelation: "Of *course* she knows. She's not *dumb*."

But the idea was too slippery to hold onto. And she could barely frame the subsequent speculation—*if* Cass knew, what then, with her prim, ladylike ways, did Cass think about it? Had she given him permission by going off? Just how bored was she?

"This is the real world out here, Leila," she said, holding Leila's eyes. "It's not like what we were raised up to expect."

Leila shrugged. "It's the real world everywhere, Cass."

"Not Alabama." Leila laughed then, and Cass gave a bright, hopeful smile. "Well, anyway, you're old enough to know what you want to do."

"I know what I *don't* want to do—does that count?"

Cass tossed her head and laughed. "Oh, then, mercy, don't do it! I'm as sorry as I can be if sending you off with Billy was a bad idea. Can't we just say we got our signals crossed? We're still neighbors, whether you like it or not. And you know Hank and I think the world of you. Let's don't fight."

"All right, Cass. But don't you all *ever* do me any more favors, okay?"

○

By now, Leila had made a plan to go to Maine during the summer, where some college friends of hers lived. She was beginning to feel she couldn't wait to get gone—to someplace stony. Someplace where the water wasn't filled with darting neon-colored fishes.

She'd been thinking lately of looking for another job for the following fall, somewhere a little more normal.

A few weeks after the party, during the week of final exams, Cass and Hank asked her to go with them to the first launching of a mutual friend's sailboat. "You'd better come on and go with us, Leila," Hank said.

"I'll let you know tomorrow. I'm just about buried in papers right now—I don't know if I'll have time."

"Hustle up and kick their butts tonight. You'll be going off next week for the whole summer—this might be the last chance you'll have to say good-bye to folks." There was a little sharp glint in the gray-blue affability of his eyes—curiosity, insinuation, inquiry.

Good-bye to which folks was what she had to ask herself. She was fairly certain that Billy Vásquez would be at this launching, too, with or without his wife. And that Cass and Hank's insistence that she go with them, whether they knew it consciously or not, had partly to do with the prospect of Billy's being there.

She thought they knew it consciously. She thought, even, that Billy might have leaned on them to deliver her.

So what? She certainly wasn't going to *hide* from him. Or from the other people likely to be there who had also been at the Plants' party that night, getting their jollies at her expense. She'd do what she wanted to do. She'd go, she'd drink rum and dance with everybody, party till all hours, right up in all their faces, then *adiós, mis amigos*. She'd be on her way to someplace where privacy was valued, where she could think about her life without all this tropical steaminess and nosiness.

Driving to the beach where the boat was to be launched, the Plants were in a keyed-up, giddy mood. It reminded Leila of the time the three of them had sat around her patio table in the middle of the night, drinking brandy in their bathrobes, the air thick with a sense of jolly collusion. Now, again, there was the confusing sense that they were in something together. Expectation, hilarity looped around her, gathering her in.

Getting their bearings, settling their gear around them, Leila and Cass at first sat on a bench together, watching a crew of eight or ten people rolling the fourteen-foot sailboat on poles across the sand toward the water's edge, Billy Vásquez among them, as she had known he would be. When he saw Cass and Leila sitting on the bench, he immediately dropped out of the group and walked across the grass toward them, shirtless, his brown lean torso unselfconsciously exposed, a gold chain with a St. Christopher medal around his neck, his wet rolled-up chinos riding low on his hips. "Hello, Cass," he said, smiling, nodding in a courtly way.

"Hello, Billy," she replied, smiling back, holding his eyes, waiting.

Then he turned to Leila, the smile fading, eyes covering her, taking her in. "And how," he asked Cass, without taking his eyes off Leila, "is your silent companion here?"

"Why don't you ask *her*?" Cass suggested.

He continued to look at Leila, his eyes moving over her face. "You should not have run away," he told her, sadly.

"No?" Leila answered. "Why's that?"

"I must speak to you—come walk with me." The look he gave her was so full of focused will (desire, you'd have to call it, she told herself, as the word formed and pulsed behind her eyes) that she felt herself pressing backward into the wooden slats of the bench to keep from being drawn straight up into it. *This day is going to be trickier than you thought*, she warned herself.

"Don't mind me," Cass said. "I was just fixin' to amble down and get a closer look at all those men."

"I don't want to speak to you, Billy," Leila said, in a voice that sounded to her own ears dogged, precise. "I want you to leave me alone."

He shook his head, abruptly, as if to clear it, but she saw that it was to dismiss what she had said. She *didn't* want him to leave her alone.

But he bowed formally and turned on his heel. As he walked back to the water, she felt his leaving as a tearing, irretrievable. *That's done it*, she thought, feeling dull and dry. *Well, good, then.* She shut her eyes against the glare, a long grim future settling around her.

"My God!" Cass said beside her, in a low, murmuring voice. "I never saw such a look in my *life*—like he wanted to burn you down." Leila heard her light a cigarette. "How could you resist him? You must be made of stone, honey child."

Leila half-opened her eyes then to glance at Cass, who, chin high, exhaled smoke in a speculative way through her full, rounded lips, her arms folded against her midriff. She turned her head toward Leila. "If you're not careful, you're going to miss a once-in-a-lifetime experience, Leila."

"How do *you* know?"

She continued to look at Leila, her brown eyes merrily suggestive. "I know about these things."

Leila looked down at the beach, where Billy now hoisted onto his shoulder the last pole the keel had cleared. She shaded her eyes to watch him take it out to the edge of the water, place it in front of the bow, then join the crew pushing the boat out over this final pole. The water lifted the keel free, the boat listed this way and that, then stabilized. Everybody cheered. Billy Vásquez looked back over his bare shoulder at Leila, smiling. She smiled back, glad—unexpectedly relieved—that her harshness would not be the final word spoken between them, that other possibilities were still open, that her future need not be as grim as all *that*.

The owner of the boat was on board now, hoisting the sails, slipping in the rudder. It was a brave boat, headed out into the harbor. Everyone would get a sail, before the day was through.

○

Later, there was a dinner at a nearby pavilion, long tables of friends drinking boisterous toasts to the boat. They roamed sociably from table to table, glasses in hand. No one stayed in one place. Leila noticed that

Van Vásquez was not among the company. Where was she? At home, waiting? What for? What *were* their arrangements? Was Billy's wife simply discounted by him, or did he hold her, in some weird way, at the center of his considerations?

Leila danced with one man, then another. She was aware of Billy's awareness of her, wherever she was.

At last Hank sat down next to her. He sighed, stretching out his tanned legs, feet in zoris. He gave them an appraising look, then rubbed his neck and looked over at her. "Now, Leila," he said, touching her arm, "I want to ask you a question."

She focused her irritation on his two fingers on her arm. "Don't," she said, fanning herself slowly with her straw hat.

"No, I just want to ask you this one thing." He gathered himself up into a sincerely interested attitude, bringing his head close to hers, looking at her, his pale eyes already slippery with alcohol. "You going to stay in that shower for the rest of your life?" She turned her head away from his heavy-lidded insinuations. "When you going to give up and join the human race?"

"The question is, Hank—" she said, looking out over the crowded dance floor, before she cut her glance back over at him, a little wildly, "—who with?"

"Well, you wouldn't want to just make do with what's handy, like everybody else in the whole world, now would you."

His sarcasm confused her. She looked out over the dance floor and for a moment she saw the tight, slow merengue going on out there in a new way. People clinging to each other, music flowing over them like time, as they moved with the beat, close to some precipice. Holding on to each other, pressing tight against each other, urgent and desperate.

"I don't know, Hank. Is that what everybody else in the whole world does?" It was an honest question, but she saw how he meant to answer it, as he stirred now to rise and gather her into the dance. She rose faster than he did, though, having drunk far less. "I'll be thinking it over," she said, over her shoulder, into his buffaloed look. She threaded her way quickly, almost in panic, through the dancers, not sure whether she was running from or toward, only that it was almost too late. She knew where she wanted to be, at the edge of things. She leaned out over the railing of the pavilion, away from the colored lights that played over the dancers, taking in deep breaths of the brackish air, looking at the water far down below, black, oily, gently lapping at the piers.

Soon Billy leaned there too, as she had known he would. His brown arm rested on the railing three inches from her own. He knew not to speak. Finally, she turned her head to take him in, to assess him; he allowed her to do so. He waited. "How can you stand it?" she asked, fiercely. "Your life, the way it is so—compromised."

"Yours is more compromised than mine, I think," he said, promptly. "You put your—standards—" he said the word as if he were trying it out for the first time, turning it up into a question—"above your feelings. This is a brutal thing."

There had been times when she would have rolled her eyes upward, at such a line as that. She did in fact laugh, but the sound shivered between them. She startled herself then, by reaching out her hand and lightly touching his lean, slightly pockmarked cheek. Just to see. To see what it would feel like, not to put her standards above her feelings. He stood looking at her attentively for a moment, poised, restrained. Then he slid his hand over hers and moved it, held it flattened against his chest. "He's married, he's *married,*" she reminded herself desperately, but it seemed a technicality, a hopeless abstraction, compared with her hand on his chest, feeling his heart's slow beat, his head ducked down toward her, his eyes on hers, drawing her up out of herself, as all her resistance, her *standards*, melted away, ran off to sea.

She couldn't take in *married*—it involved thinking of a third person, and now she could think only of two.

He turned her, eventually, into his arms. The hoarse, reckless singing, as if it had worn itself out in wild lament, was the only speaking between them. For a moment she felt as she had when she danced with him on the Plants' porch, as though a spotlight were trained on them, as though everyone, *todo el mundo*, were watching what was happening between them—entertaining themselves with the big seduction, she said to herself. Only she could not have said with certainty, at this point, the music molding them into one exact body, for all intents, which one of them was seducing the other. Cass slid her shining brown eyes over the shoulder of the owner of the sailboat and caught Leila's. Leila registered Cass's smile—teasing, flattering. Complicit.

Her perceptions then seemed to be dilating, like the pupils of the eye, so that the outer world blurred, fuzzed out, and in a moment she was not aware of anyone, only of herself. And him. She had never felt so—attended to. He held her, moving and still, in the dark, until the music ended.

Then, he put his hand to her elbow to guide her quickly through the crowd, out of the pavilion, toward his car. He opened the door for her, got in on the other side, reached into his pocket for the key, looking somewhat shaken himself. "We'll go to the inn at the end of the road, shall we?"

"No," she said. "Come home with me."

"But—" He looked at her, hand arrested in the act of turning the key in the ignition. "Are you sure?" he asked, smiling.

"I don't care." And then she thought to ask, quickly, "Do you?"

He hesitated for just long enough to meet her eyes, a little flash of conjecture entering his smile, then disappearing. He started the engine, backed the car around, and sped down the sand road onto the highway.

They drove along the coast, and then up past the town of American banks and *supermercados* and four-lane highways, into the hills above the university. Up the drive through the great overgrown hedges of poinsettia to the terraced pink house, floating in a sea of jasmine. He backed his car in behind hers, leaving the Plants' place free for them. When he shut off the engine, the *coquís'* song rushed in.

She unlocked her front door. The moon shined down through the louvers so beautifully that she would not have turned on the light in any case. She led him across the tiles toward the bed where she had awakened so often in loneliness and terror.

As when she danced with him, the feeling of being taught remained. The feeling of having danced before in her life, but not really. *Nobody knows these things*, she surfaced once, above him, to think. *Or maybe everybody knows them, has always known them. Everybody but me.* This thought crossed her mind, to be followed by no other. He vaporized thought. He knew how. It was outside her previous experience of sex—urgent helpless hurry, clothes flying, bodies sliding on a tide of passion and proximity, not bad but not this. This was a dance, a complex game, with rules that had been worked out over centuries in some secret society, passed down to the chosen—first have all night before you, first be in no hurry, first learn restraint. It was a ceremony. And a favor, yes, a great favor someone was doing for you—first do this and then do that, then with delicate decisiveness move on, until there was absolutely nothing left of your honored partner but a fever, a pulse.

So that when the sound came that she thought she expected, she didn't even hear it, and didn't at first recognize it when she did hear it, the turning wheels crunching the gravel. They were both arrested, brought up out of their glazed, mesmerized state by it. He looked at her through the darkness—from a distance, it seemed, a waiting distance—as the car doors slammed and the quick footsteps came across the gravel.

Now, the soft slip-slap of zoris on the concrete terrace, past the closed door of her bedroom, and then her bedroom window. The closed curtains stirred toward the bed. Neither of them moved or breathed.

The dream she'd had that night when Hank brought the woman home flitted disturbingly through her mind.

The self-conscious, tipsy footsteps mounted the stairs. The screened door slapped shut. The floor above them creaked. "They're tiptoeing," she said—it was the first thing either of them had said since entering the house. She glanced at him, hoping he'd laugh.

"Yes," he said, not giving anything away. "They are very considerate, Cass and Hank." Leila remembered Cass's smile at her over her partner's shoulder that evening. Intimate, suggestive. Recommending, yes. Knowing.

How do you *know*?

Oh, I know about these things.

Billy looked at her quietly, waiting. If she asked him a direct question, he would answer it. But what business was it of hers? And then, as he gathered her to the game again, she forgot the question, forgot the Plants, forgot everything she had ever known. Let it all slip away from her, right out of her grasp.

He lay on his back, then, smoking. "You must move from here. When you return. To somewhere with much movement—the old town, perhaps. You need to be able to have your life, without—interested neighbors."

Later, stirring out of a slender sleep, she murmured, "I didn't want to turn to stone."

"Oh!" he said, deeply concerned, drawing her to him to show her that turning to stone was the last thing in the world she needed to worry about.

Near dawn, she watched him as he dressed in the dark, removed now from her into his own life. And as she watched him drawing his shirt over his head, she felt she could *see* his life, how it went, his many affairs—she knew there had been many, not so much because it would have taken a lot of practice to develop such expertise; it was more that if you had this gift, this instinct, you would of course be drawn, over and over, to those who inspired you to express it.

He glanced up, saw her watching him, came to sit beside her on the edge of the bed. As though overcoming shyness, they moved their heads at the same moment, looked each other in the eye.

"Are you glad for this night?" he asked her, seriously. It was not a rhetorical question.

"*Now* I'm glad." She gave a breath of a laugh. "I expect to be sorry later."

He did not register, or else did not credit, her ironic tone. "Never be sorry," he whispered, in his husky, sweet, Latin voice. "Not for this, Leila. For the waste, before—all the times, wasted." He stood and pulled her up, fit his hands flat against hers, lining them up, palm to palm, finger to finger. They were shaped alike, pale against dark. "You must really leave next week?"

"Yes."

He nodded, bringing her hands up now on either side of his neck. "I wish—I wish we had discovered ourselves sooner."

She shook her head. "It would have been impossible."

"No," he said flatly, drawing her close, so that his shirt pressed against her bare skin. "We would have found a way to make it possible. And it would have been better for you."

"Better for me?"

"Than nights of loneliness. Imagining thieves breaking in."

"Oh!"

She backed up a step, smiling hard, feeling tears burning in her eyes, seeing how Hank—or Cass—must have told him. Told everybody. How they all must have known the story of her screaming for help in the night, and what it meant. Must have known it that night when they chanted *Leila goes along*. Everybody doing her a favor, even Billy's wife. And tonight, too—it wasn't her imagination, everybody had watched him dance her into a trance. *For all to see*, she kept thinking: they must have looked at her and imagined (with a little thrill) what the night held for the woman who had screamed for help, the sex-starved woman who had put her head down on her arms and cried. *Oh honey, help is on its way.*

She sat on the bed, then abruptly lay down on it, covered herself entirely with the sheet, dumb with humiliation. He sat down again beside her, gently uncovering her face. He was not smiling, as she had thought he would be; his eyes were lambent, wet-looking in the darkness. "Leila—" He combed her hair back from her temples. "No one—no one thought anything. Except that it was—regrettable. For you, a woman like you. To be alone."

Tears slid down the sides of her face. He brushed them away with his thumbs, gently, holding her face between his hands. "This has not been an easy place for you."

And then: "Will we see each other again?" he asked. "Before you leave?"

Island nights, she thought, as though she had already lost them. The frogs were screaming, the leaves rustled in the wind. The thinning darkness was filled with riot, with fragrant, excited confusion.

In a few days, she would fly away from this island on a plane filled with tanned tourists, well-satisfied with their vacations. She would not return in the fall, she knew that now. She looked into the face so close above her in the dark, taut with intention. Billy Vásquez, the once-in-a-lifetime experience.

What was handy.

She took a breath—the soft dawn breeze was filled, as always, with the perfume of jasmine. It was what she would remember most clearly, when she was gone from here. She freed one arm from the sheet and reached up to trace his full, smooth lower lip with her fingertip. "Will we see each other again before you leave?" he had asked. And now he watched her closely, seriously, waiting for an answer.

So she smiled and shrugged.

"*¿Cómo no?*" she said.

Advanced Beginners

ADVANCED BEGINNERS

Jana dreamed at night of half-mown fields. Of foxtail, other blond weeds, going down behind her. A wake of stubble that from a distance looked green, the neat, definite green margins widening. "The mown world," she said once, in company, meaning *the known world*. Maybe she'd been on the tractor too long. But it was true; where the mower had passed, the land seemed discovered. She could see its shape, its conformation.

Also, its condition: no grass to speak of, thorn and cedar and sumac thickets, millions of rocks. Two ponds that didn't seem to hold water. Any fool could have seen. She hadn't asked anybody for advice; she had just laid her money down.

But the problems weren't insolvable. *Someday.* She carried the word around in her pocket, as she carried the farm around in her pocket, and went on mowing. Counting her blessings: the herd of serviced cows, almost enough wood for the winter, the old Ford tractor. And the thirty-year mortgage on the house and the hundred and eighty acres that went with it.

When she turned off the tractor motor in the barn, she felt its vibrations still in the palms of her hands. The high drifts of pure bright purple kept circling toward her. An ocean of ironweed.

A week after she'd seen this place for the first time, she'd sold the bonds she had inherited from her grandmother, in order to finance the down payment and buy the small herd of cattle and the tractor. A month later, she had quit her job as assistant to a landscape architect and moved in. She could scrape along for a year, she calculated, on her savings and what she'd made leasing out the tobacco allotment. Then what would happen? "Jesus, Jana, of all times to be buying a farm," Luke, her sometime lover and spiritual advisor, had said. "You need your head examined. Why didn't you just hire a plane and throw dollar bills out over Oxford County?"

She would sell her first calves early next spring. She planned to raise her next tobacco allotment herself, not lease it out, see how that went. If she had to go back to work to keep the place, she would. She'd do whatever she could, and hope it was enough.

She wanted to stay. Her only physical attachment now was to the things that surrounded her here. The woodstove, for instance. One day, as the fall came in earnest, she found herself standing with her arms around the stovepipe—not touching it, of course, but meaning some kind of embrace, overcome by its faithfulness, its dear silent companionship, the way it kept putting out gentle heat long after she had left the room. On the side of the stove was a motto, in Norwegian, meaning something like: *I pray to God that my fire never goes out.*

Against that possibility, she hugged the new calves when their mothers weren't looking and often kissed the huge old bur oak growing down by the creek. She was in love with this place and with her life in it.

She hadn't understood at first that she was looking for a farm, when, the previous November, she had begun driving around by herself a few evenings a week, after work, following the narrower fork of every road, happiest when she no longer knew where she was.

The first time she was late getting home, Luke had looked up from the stack of essays he was reading. "Where were you?" he asked, mildly curious, not at all accusatory.

"Out in the country. Lost."

"Where were you trying to go?" he asked, getting ready to help her discover where she went wrong.

"Nowhere in particular." He looked at her with his kind, teacherly eyes that seemed to be waiting always for her to go on, to express herself more clearly. These expectations of his made her nervous. She didn't want to know the world in the orderly way he knew it. "I was just driving around," she offered clumsily. "Sightseeing, I guess."

One February evening, she had stopped and backed up past an overgrown tree line to look again at an old square frame house set down in a creek bottom, the wooded hills and overgrown fields rising up all around it. She hadn't seen the For Sale sign, fallen sideways in the tall weeds, until she started forward again.

"Just something that happened," Luke said, explaining to her why she was leaving him, trying to be generous, trying to absolve her. She had sat clutching her coffee cup tightly with both hands, watching his lips move, taking note of his tone, loving and philosophical. But it had seemed then, as it seemed now, that he was also describing how she had taken up with him, describing her whole meandering life, until that moment. *Just something that happened.* She wished to learn another way of moving forward. By intuition and instinct and clear desire.

She saw that it might have been that wish, not yet quite formulated, that had led her, at about the same time she had taken to driving around the countryside, to enroll in a ballet class. She hadn't been willing to give up the dancing once she'd moved out to the farm, even though she often felt at the limits of her physical endurance by the end of a day of running the tractor or mucking out the barn. Two nights a week, she would take a fast shower, pull on her leotard and sweatpants, and drive the thirty miles to Lexington, in order to teach her body to gather itself and at the same time propel itself through a sequence of movements. To *move*, not meander.

○

When she looked in the mirror these days, she saw a new face, earnest, unadorned. She reminded herself of an adolescent boy, with squared shoulders and wind-chapped lips and alert dark eyes, full of questions.

She didn't exactly miss Luke, but her chest sometimes felt sore, as though she'd had surgery, as though something in there had been removed.

She had spent much of her time through the summer and early fall simply clearing things out—the detritus of a series of no-account tenants, leaving in a hurry. She hauled away abandoned cars, rusted machinery, trash heaps; she hired a bulldozer to push in a half-dozen little mudhole ponds that had been dug in impossible places. She cleared thorn tree thickets, tore out patchy wire fences that cut through the original set of fields.

When at last she was able to see the basic organization of the farm, it seemed obvious, inevitable. But as she grew more familiar with it, and with the necessities of farming, she began to understand what it must have looked like to its first owner, who had received it as a Revolutionary War grant—a series of forested ridges, dropping this way and that to the long creek meadow, which widened and curved and narrowed in response to the ridges' way of meeting it. She came to respect the intelligence, the eye for things, the aesthetic practicality of the one who'd carved these particular fields, rather than any other, out of the woods, chosen where to place the barns, the fences, the wagon roads, the house. Someone had known exactly what to do with this unruly land; she felt that someone had loved it as much as she did, but more expertly.

Originally, the farm had been in the hands of a family named Carpenter; she had traced the deed. Burgess Carpenter had been the last one; he'd died almost thirty years before. Since then, the farm had changed hands ten times. But everyone still called it the Carpenter Place. "You want them to call it something else," said Harry Lucas, who was hanging his tobacco in her barn that fall in exchange for hay, "you'll have to stay awhile." He glanced at her and smiled, but only a little. "I'd say fifty, sixty years ought to do it."

When he said that, she shivered—for she saw her life, then, as though she had stopped on the wagon road that curved into the cedar woods to look back at herself, a long time before, standing by the barn, kicking a clump of burdock, talking to Harry Lucas.

Out mowing along the fence lines, or cleaning out the rocked-in spring with the beech trees all around it, or repairing the cattle guard that ran across the creek, she thought about the Carpenters—Burgess, who'd been born and raised here, and the ones before him.

The house had a reputation for being haunted. She'd never seen the ghost herself, but sometimes at night when she sat reading her bulletins from the Extension Service, her books on pasture management, a man would come into her mind, as though she were *remembering* him, long-shanked and stiffly angular, kneeling, in a green cap, to pound stakes into the hard ground with the blunt end of a hatchet. Or thumbing ten-dollar bills carefully out of his wallet, counting to himself. She saw his old, splayed thumb sliding the new bills forward.

Burgess Carpenter had raised cattle, corn, and goats, Harry Lucas said. And apples—there had been an apple orchard on the hill above the house, she could tell from the old aerial photograph. She was thinking of starting a new orchard in the same place.

She asked Harry if there had ever been a cemetery on the farm.

He looked at her cautiously. She was afraid he was worried about her. His eyes had dark marks under the inside corners, like little smudges, as though he for one had no trouble seeing ghosts. Those marks, and the stringent jawline and flat cheeks, gave his face a permanent seriousness, an air of deep concentration. "Once there was one grave—that's all the cemetery I ever heard of on this place, Burgess Carpenter's. But it's gone now."

"Gone?" she asked in alarm. "Gone where?"

He glanced at her, then folded his arms and shifted his eyes to study the ground, as though this conversation embarrassed him a little. "Well, what happened was, when he found out he was dying he went on home from the doctor's office and built himself a coffin. He came and got my dad and showed him where he wanted it to go—he had it all measured and staked out the way he wanted to lay. Facing west. He made Daddy promise to dig the hole and get him into it right away, when the time came. 'Before they get to doing their monkeyshines over me.' That's what he said." He glanced up at her with his matter-of-fact green eyes. "His children, he was meaning—they were all gone off one place and another by then, but not far enough to suit him. He didn't have no use for them because they'd all left the farm behind."

"He lived here alone?"

"By the time I came along, he did. His wife died early, before I was born. It was always just Burgess over here, when I was a boy. His kids had left by then, too."

All the solitary men in this country—Harry Lucas, too. You had the feeling every one of them had resisted the general tendency toward leaving at some great private cost. Harry was grave, dogged, devoted to his work. He reminded her of a monk.

"Anyway, my daddy dug the grave, but old Burgess wasn't in it long enough to get comfortable. This one daughter from Cincinnati heard what he'd done with himself and came tearing down and called in the law. She missed the lowering, but she sure made it to the raising up. He's over at the cemetery in Ellenburg now. No wonder he wanders around, poor old fella—he don't know where his body's at."

"Have you seen him?"

He looked up at her with a surprised laugh.

○

That night, in dance class, the Brandenburg Concerto no. 3 tumbled over them, resonating through their heels. Dave walked quickly to the front of the dim, spotlit studio. "All right, second!" he cried, turning to face them, and brought his own body into it, arms down, hands exact. "And now, reach! Reach up! And again!" Jana's torso stretched thin, out of the area of willpower and muscle tone at last, into something else, pure desire. Dave moved among them, his hand pressing once, hard, down a spine, or smoothing a shoulder blade upward with his palm. He paused before Jana, probing under her rib cage with three fingers. "Lift, lift the chest and let it carry you—" quickly back in front of the class again, showing them "—down."

Some of the other students were incredibly limber, could bend from the hips and practically lay a forearm along the floor. Not Jana.

Luke had been right, of course, when he told her she needed to stretch out before she took ballet lessons. She was obsessed now. She wanted to be strong enough to lift a hay bale with one arm, but she also wanted to have these extravagant movements at her command, not to be stopped somewhere along the way by something that wouldn't give.

Dave was showing them the new progression of steps, the chassé, the falling back, the turn. "A good straight look," he told them. "A decisive motion."

It was her turn across the floor. A strong, abrupt movement into the chassé, head high, back arched—so far, so good. "Beautiful, Jana!" Dave shouted. She sailed across the floor, her arms precise, fluid, effortless. But now came the next part; in the sudden pivot, her body grew confused. Dave ran out to do it with her. "Fall back now through the foot, and then the shoulders stop it. Look out there, beyond your arm. Look right out there, like you've made up your mind. And now the turn," he said, extending through all his long leg and bare foot.

She couldn't get it, couldn't get it—"Oh, what's *wrong*?"

"You're going to have to content yourself with smaller movements for the time being," Dave told her kindly, his arm around her shoulders. "Don't try to fake it—that's how people get hurt."

"It doesn't work, anyhow," he went on.

○

The next time Burgess Carpenter came into her mind, he was measuring lumber. Some of those old cedar boards she'd found way back in the loft of the barn. He threw one aside, slid another one out, sighted down it, wrote on it, then stuck his pencil behind his ear.

One day when she was waiting for her truck to be worked on,

she walked over to the Ellenburg Municipal Cemetery and found his grave. It was marked by a respectable, ordinary stone, shiny granite, with a rectangle set in for the name and dates, *January 11, 1890–August 15, 1969.*

He'd known just where he wanted to be and had told Harry Lucas's father. He'd built his coffin and made his arrangements. But it hadn't done him any good. He'd ended up here, between the hospital and the Ford dealership.

When she walked on the farm, she would come to a stop sometimes—on the grassy hillock atop the highest ridge, or down in a ferny clearing of the oak woods: *Is this the place he chose?* she would wonder. *Or this?* She wished she could dig him up again and bring him back. He'd known just where he wanted to be.

○

The trees were swinging one way, then another. They made Jana think of choirs of black gospel singers. Something at the same time fixed and wild in the way they took the wind. Or, as her neighbor Dippy Zoony now observed, spitting over his shoulder contemplatively: "Weather has a lot of charisma, you know?"

D.Z. Hites, another solitary man: cattle and tobacco farmer, odd-job hustler, philosopher, ex-con. Snow on the lenses of his granny glasses. One of her major human contacts these days. Been to Eddyville Penitentiary and Tucson, Arizona. Come home again. Dizzy Heights, Harry Lucas called him.

"What were you up for, D.Z.?" she asked him in a comradely tone, as they climbed the hill together.

"When I'm drunk, I'm crazy," he answered cheerfully. "Whew," he said, shaking his head in disbelief and pride.

She and D.Z. had something in common—his steers, who

wandered through his so-called fence into her bottom pasture every other day. He never noticed. His phone had been disconnected for two or three weeks, so if she wanted him to help her herd them back onto his place, she had to drive over to his house, with its rotted-out front porch and torn curtains hanging out the second-story window. He always dropped whatever he was doing and came right along, zipping up his jacket and smiling his coy, gallant smile, under the impression that what she was really after was his hulking body.

"You're really going to have to fix your fence, D.Z.," she said now, sternly, into the wind that lashed around them. "I'm not kidding. I'm sick of this—it's too cold. Anyway, I'm planning to turn my herd in here next week."

He gave her the eye. "I believe you're a real cow mother in your heart. I believe you *love* them old cows of yours."

"I do, you're right. And I don't want your steers in here churning up the field and making a lot of trouble."

"You got to mellow down a little bit, Janalee. Now trust old Dr. D.Z." He put his hand in its thick glove over his chest, giving her a sweet, small-eyed smile. "When I say I'll do a thing, I'll do it." She looked at him skeptically. "I mean that sincerely. I'm a man of my word."

"Sincerely?" she said.

He laughed. "I'm a real sincere kind of fellow, didn't you know, Jana? It's my main strength." He chucked her chin with his padded knuckle. "I thought that was why you liked me."

She stared at him. "Fix your damn fence, D.Z."

At first, she had thought she was the next thing to invisible out here, but—thanks to D.Z.'s coy intimations—she'd begun to understand that she was the object of fairly dirty speculation out at the gas station at the interchange. ("These old boys out here, it hurts their feelings to see a small woman trying to handle an ax. Maybe if you had some *heft* to you they wouldn't mind so much. I know one or two that was wanting to come on out and get you started good. But I said, just leave the lady alone. Janalee likes to do things for herself." Poker-faced, except for the little gleeful insinuations behind the round lenses. "I'm doing right to tell them that, ain't I, Jana? That you like to do things for yourself?") Everybody out here knew that she was a woman without a man; it was only natural that they should wonder why—she wondered why herself—and what she was doing at night, all by herself, in such a barn of a house, big enough for a family of ten. One night, when she answered the telephone, a hoarse, drunken voice on the other end had bawled out an angry taunt of which she hadn't understood anything but the last words, *horny bitch.* She hung up the phone then, genuinely bewildered, wondering if somebody out there in the night knew something about her that *she* didn't know. Not D.Z.—D.Z. was on parole and in AA. But, she thought, somebody who'd heard about her from D.Z. Or maybe the caller had just dialed her number at random.

○

"The back's got to be electric," Dave said, facing the dancers in the studio. "If the back's dead, *every*thing's dead." Jana could bend her body, now, into a right angle, hinged at the hips. In that position she could round her back, then suddenly make it long and straight again. It had taken months and months—but she felt that her back was showing signs of life; she could see that the movement from curve to elongation was beautiful. She watched herself in the long mirror, doing deep, careful second-position pliés in the long mirror. She brought her leg straight up and then out.

It wasn't dancing, but it was the beginning of dancing. Some of the people in her class moved on to Intermediate. Others dropped out. What Jana did was to stay behind, because she knew her limitations. She wasn't ever going to be a real dancer—but she was confident she had what it took to be a true Advanced Beginner.

On the farm, she was doing a different dance. The dance of pure necessity. She brought the ax up and started it downward, letting it fall of its own weight, bringing her knees into its momentum. *A good straight look, a decisive motion.* That much, at least. The hickory log fell open in its bright clear grain, or the ax hung, and she would have to kick the stubborn log away from the blade. She climbed into the bed of the truck and forked out hay for the cows. She scouted the hill in foot-deep snow, looking for the newborn calf, the bull calf with its thick, sturdy legs.

No, not *pure* necessity, though this was the dead of winter now. There were flights of fancy, even so. The deer on the crest of the ridge became aware of her. Jana dropped to the ground on the slope below, downwind. The young doe paused, brought her head up on its eloquent, wavering neck, lifted her nostrils; then, not alarmed, just to be on the safe side, she turned and trotted down the other slope, made a little leap, sheer exuberance, then leapt again. At last, in no particular hurry, she sailed over the fence, her jaunty white flag disappearing through the woods on the other side. Five young squirrels played on the icy branches of the sugar tree by the barn, sliding, slipping, swinging by their forepaws, scrambling up again, never falling. *All things join in the dance.* She'd found the words in a book of medieval songs. *Ye who dance not know not what we are knowing. Amen.*

When she broke the ice in the stock tank, when she climbed to the loft to throw down bales of hay, when she jumped the icy creek or bent to hitch the wagon to the tractor, she was conscious that her body was reiterating the movements of Burgess Carpenter's body, and of bodies long before his. He had known all these steps; she felt he was handing them down to her. He might have been a terrible man—maybe he drove his children away by his cruelty or irascibility. But in her mind, he was the last hero of this piece of land. She felt herself to be his student, his heir.

She was growing lean and muscular, from the dancing, and from her work. Long indentations had appeared on either side of her tight stomach.

But she was chaste. She lived alone in a haunted house, enfolded now by drafts from the floor, from the cracks around the windows and doors. She went around stuffing insulation into the places she had missed back in August, coming across little drifts of snow behind the books in the bookcase, between the top and bottom sashes of the windows, on the pantry shelf.

She drove the tractor up toward the barn, watching Harry Lucas loading baled tobacco onto his truck, to take to market, admiring his supple shoulders, his authoritative, easy movements. But her admiration seemed not to yearn toward completion, toward any kind of *having*. What she felt was a kind of naturalist's ecstasy. Removed, off at a bird-watcher's distance. A wave of desolation, emptiness came over her then. Was it going to be this way from now on?

She turned off the motor, climbed down from the tractor. He came out of the stripping room once again and closed the door behind him this time, zipping his jacket. He stopped and turned toward her, until she caught up with him, then fell into step beside her, his hands in his pockets. They walked up the farm road together from the barn to his truck. She knew he had waited for her; she felt tongue-tied, empty-handed. He looked down at her. "Snow on the way again."

She nodded. "So I heard," she said shyly.

They walked on a few more steps, stopped beside the door of his truck. "You know," he said carefully, squinting over her shoulder, "it's almost all weather out here." He shifted his green eyes sideways to meet hers then, to see if she was with him. "What it did and what it *might* do. There ain't much else."

"There's cows," she said, smiling.

"Cows and weather," he said, smiling himself, but grimly, as though he really believed it.

"That's enough, right there."

The lines on either side of his mouth eased out of the smile for a second, as he looked at her, to see how she meant that, and she had to back up a step, away from his clear, frank gaze, because she didn't know herself how she meant it. She put her hands in her jacket pockets and shrugged.

He saw her confusion; for a second his eyes continued to hold hers, drawing up through her body all her austere, lonely life. "Well, sometimes it is, sometimes it ain't," he remarked then, pleasantly. His eyes dropped, out of politeness or his own shyness, to study the little hollow between her collarbones. She felt undefended, exposed, as though her pulse were visible there. When he met her eyes again, the smile was still there, but a definite question had entered into it.

"Right now," she said, "right now, cows and weather are about all I can handle." And then, because she couldn't bear the conclusive sound of those words, she went on, out of control, astonishing herself: "Maybe it'll be different in the spring."

He still looked at her, for a moment, out of his light eyes with the bruised-looking places underneath, not letting her off. Then he roused himself and turned, stepped up into his truck. "You got to hope so," he said wryly, before he closed the door. When he had turned the truck and started down the drive, she lifted her hand in a wave. He waved back, or rather raised his open hand, like a man swearing to tell the truth.

Coldhearted, she called herself then, turning up the driveway, kicking viciously at the gravel. Heartless, sexless. But that was something outside of herself talking to her—the men at the gas station. What she *really* felt was that she was in the grip of some grave process; she had to follow it through; everything else would have to wait. She yanked the cord of the chain saw, then yanked it again. She moved methodically among the limbs of the oak tree that had fallen into the field. She loaded the cut lengths into the wagon, then started the saw up again.

○

The stove's red coil was the only light in the room. The milk rose in the pot to its silent boil. She caught it just as it started over the edge of the pot, poured it into her cup. She was all right. It had only been a dream.

Nightmares came out of periods of change, someone had told her.

She turned off the stove; the red coil faded. In the dark, she found her way to the chair, sat down, and opened the vent of the woodstove. The stovepipe tapped, heating up—Burgess Carpenter at the door.

No, she'd never see him, not really, only in her mind. Only what she could imagine. But her imagining had a psychic edge to it, she knew—she'd seen him driving the stakes into the ground before Harry had told her how he had picked out the place where he wanted to be buried, for instance. This knowledge didn't frighten her, but she didn't know what to make of it.

She got up and turned on the porch light, so that she could watch the snow falling, through the window of the back door. When she'd gone to bed, there had been just a fine dust of snow drifting down, but now a blizzard had settled in.

The cold drove her quickly back to the stove. She held her blanket against her, so that the folds at the back wouldn't scorch.

She only remembered her dreams when they woke her; she wished they wouldn't wake her. She felt sleep-deprived. She drank her milk and watched the window of the door. The flakes of snow came through the light thickly, at their oblique slant. Then a face came, too—a whole torso, but it wasn't Burgess Carpenter, it was a young woman, in a green quilted jacket, banging on the window-pane with her bare knuckles. She wore no cap. Her hair was wild, snow caught in it.

Jana turned on the lamp, opened the door. They stared at each other in mutual blank alarm for a second. Then the girl pulled herself up and said, "I ran off the road up there." Her face was bright, painfully flushed.

"Come on in." Jana stood back, and the girl entered the room. Nylon hose, pumps with little heels, Jana couldn't believe it. "Oh, you poor thing! Your feet must be frozen." The girl looked down at her feet, interested. Her stockings were black, to match her fashionable gaucho pants that ended four inches above the ankle. "Come by the stove; I'll get you some wool socks."

"That's all right." She sat down in the rocking chair and put her left foot in her lap, began rubbing it.

"What about some coffee, something hot to drink?"

"I took out some of your fence up there at the top of the hill. That's still your farm up there, I guess." Her voice had a quick, flat strum to it.

"Don't worry about it," Jana said, but thought in dismay of her cows and calves, probably out roaming the countryside already.

"I started out to D.Z.'s, but I saw your light, so I thought I'd better just try to get this far. Then I got afraid nobody'd be here. I don't know what I would've done then." She looked at her foot as she rubbed it, then up at Jana through her bangs. "Broke in, I guess." The snow was melting in her thick, dark-brown hair now. She ran her fingers through it, shook it back. Her face had something smooth and incipient in it, something on the brink, Jana thought, in the broad cheekbones, the high-bowed smooth lips. A pretty girl, well taken care of, her green jacket stitched in a fancy expensive department-store pattern, a pair of antique silver earrings with small diamonds in them dangling primly from her ears. Recently an Oxford County cheerleader, by the look of her, or maybe there was something a little too steamy about her for that, nineteen or so now, carefully made up for wandering around in a blizzard at two a.m., with bronze eye shadow and long painted fingernails. "I'm Sherry Willoughby. My daddy's Buck Willoughby," she volunteered, with an air of putting Jana's mind at ease. "He'll fix y'all's fence. We live out on 27. Somebody's always going through *our* fence. Half of them never even offer to pay."

"That's all right. It wasn't much fence to start with."

"He'll come and take care of it. Tomorrow morning, if I know *him*."

She seemed intent on it, so Jana said, "Okay. Thanks. That's nice of you."

The girl nodded and, having gotten this business out of the way, gave herself over to an abrupt shudder.

"Here," Jana commanded, feeling maternal. "Put this blanket around you." The girl seemed more to submit to this attention than to accept it. Jana got her parka down from its nail by the door and put it on over her flannel nightgown. "What happens now?" she asked. "I'll take you home if you want me to."

"I just need to use your phone," Sherry said. She stood up, letting the blanket fall around her feet, and then, silver bracelets clinking down her wrist, she seemed to be trying to find something in the pocket of her jacket. She brought out a handful of scraps of paper. Most of them drifted to the floor, along with some disintegrating pieces of Kleenex.

She looked down at them in puzzlement, and Jana realized for the first time that the girl had been drinking, the faint sweet reek of whiskey hovering around the edges of her perfume. Jana watched her kneel and pick up one slip of paper, look at it front and back, put it in her pocket, then pick up another. "I can't find it," she said, in the same flat, direct voice. "I had it." But her hands were trembling. She stood up, seeming to forget about the confetti at her feet. The two of them looked at each other straight on for the first time since Jana had opened the door. They were almost the same height. Sherry blew the hair out of her eyes and threw her head back, as if to let Jana see that she was still in command of her situation. "Have you got a phone book?"

"Sure." Jana gave it to her, and the girl stared, dazed, at the page she'd opened it to, as though she'd remember the alphabet in a minute. "You want me to look something up for you?"

"I guess I'm a little shook up. I'm wanting to call D.Z. He'll come after me."

"His phone's disconnected."

"It is?"

"Yes."

She looked down at the book uncertainly, then offered it back to Jana abruptly. "Maybe I could make it over there now."

"I'll drive you there. Or take you on home, if you want—maybe that'd be better. I'm not sure D.Z.'s there—I didn't see his light on tonight, I don't think."

Sherry spread her hands out to the stove. "If you could maybe just run me over there. I'm sure he's there." She looked at her narrow red-nailed hands as if in a trance. "He *said* he'd be." She glanced at Jana then, startled, a small, involuntary smile lifting one corner of her mouth. There was a moment when Jana thought they were both going to laugh out loud, but then the girl almost visibly decided on a straight face. "D.Z.'s a real good friend of mine," she explained. "His sister was my best friend in high school. Do you know Kelly?"

"No. I only know D.Z."

"Kelly's at Eastern now. She's going to be a pharmacist. We've all been friends most all our lives. D.Z.'s a real good person to talk to. At least for me," she went on. "He's pretty smart, even if he got himself in trouble that one time. He's straight now. He won't even take a beer." She seemed to run out of energy, ended wistfully, "He's always been real good to me."

Jana nodded, trying to give her the benefit of the doubt. What else could she do? Say *Stay away from him, honey, he's not good enough for you*? Tell her how she'd finally had to just about rebuild his whole back fence herself? How would her daddy, the responsible Buck Willoughby, like that? The middle of the night, a blizzard going on, and this girl had put on her diamond earrings, belted down a few drinks, and taken off to see D.Z. *Any time.* Jana could hear his intimate, sinusy voice. A real good person to talk to—God! "I'll put on some clothes," she murmured. "And then I'll run you over there."

Jana went into the bedroom and pulled on over her nightgown a pair of Luke's castoff corduroy pants and a heavy sweater, then her coveralls and snow boots, because she thought there was a chance she'd be chasing cows before this night was over. She caught a glimpse of herself in the dim mirror and wondered what her grandmother would think—Jana thought of her suddenly, Granny Crump, showing her the lingerie cases she was making out of scraps of satin. "Now, I'm making these for all the girls. Don't you want one too, Janalee? They're sweet, I think—for when you go off to college." The quick old veined fingers against the pink satin. "We could put a sprig of lavender in this net pocket. Or some rose petals."

The girl looked at Jana in polite amazement when she came back into the kitchen, stuffing her hair under her red wool cap.

In the truck, Sherry settled back. "I like the way your house is fixed up," she said, making conversation. "It's real pretty."

"I still have a lot to do."

"You live there alone?" she ventured, after a minute.

"Yeah."

"Oh." Sherry nodded seriously and clasped her hands tightly in her lap. Then, as if glad to be able to change this painful subject, she said, brightly, "There's my car."

Jana had expected to see the car sort of off in a ditch, but it was twenty feet out in the field, having run off the road miraculously at the one flat ridgetop. More miraculously than that, it had come to rest right where the ridge broke and began its sharp decline. "I'll *say* you ran off the road." The snow on the road was still fairly dry, blowing—there'd been no traffic, and there was no slickness yet. She must have been driving forty-five miles an hour on this narrow, twisting lane to have come so far out of the curve. "I don't know why you didn't turn over," she couldn't help saying.

"If I'd gone ten more feet, I would have been dead, I guess," Sherry said, in her abrupt, factual voice. "I left the radiator up there in the fence. All the chrome's tore off. I was just about to take it in to get it fixed up—two more years and it would have been a classic." At this her voice trembled, unexpectedly. She put her hands in her pockets, and then she was crying, in a ladylike, silent way, her shoulders shaking. "I could have killed myself out there," she said. And then, "I'm having a real hard time right now."

"Oh, I'm sorry," Jana said, trying to rise to the occasion. "What's wrong?"

"I guess—" the girl wiped her eyes carefully with the heel of her hand"—I guess I just need to talk to D.Z."

Jana pulled up in front of his dark house. "I'll wait," she told her. "In case you can't raise him."

Sherry nodded distractedly and slid out, then leaned back in and said, "I'll get a tow truck to haul that car out of your field first thing tomorrow. Thanks for everything, hear?"

She went up on the front porch. Jana zipped up her jacket and waited. The girl looked so vulnerable, unsparingly illuminated by the security light, standing there in her designer pants on the planks D.Z. had laid across the rotten joists, the dogs barking all around her. The door opened at last. There was D.Z., in a pair of blue jeans and an unbuttoned shirt. Sherry turned and waved at Jana. D.Z., without his glasses, squinted over her shoulder, curious and little-eyed as a possum. Then the girl stepped into the dark house and the door closed. Old Hard-Times Doctor D.Z. *I'm a real sincere kind of fella. It's my main strength.* He'd go right to stroking the girl's hair. *Whatever you want,* he'd say. *Whatever you think would be good for you.* Leading her sincerely toward the bedroom. Somewhere under that roof there was bound to be a water bed. Mediterranean, with mirrors. Jana almost, for a second, felt it undulate as D.Z. lowered his hefty body onto it. *God!* she thought, and then, *Who asked* you? She put the car in gear and turned around.

Cows' faces in the headlights. White Foot, Short Legs, and their two calves, right in the middle of the road. She backed up past the place where the fence was out and turned the truck across the road as a barrier. Then she got out and circled behind the little band, to cluck them gently along. They went forward in disarray, but turned mildly back into the fields at the gap in the fence. She pulled her truck up then, to block the gap.

The moon was full, but under clouds. Somehow there was light, anyway, as if it came out of the snow. The wind had dropped; the snow floated down in heavy, dreamy flakes, a kind of whisper inside the still air. She saw the rest of the herd: a still, dark configuration against the snow down by the creek. The road cows ran toward it, their calves trundling behind them, trying to keep up. Jana followed and counted heads, just to be sure she'd gotten them all back in the field. Everyone was there but the big yellow ringleader, Hera. Jana walked along the frozen creek and finally saw her, off on the other side, in the cedars, snow coating her wide back. She'd pick a night like this to calve, Hera would. Jana would have to come back out in a few hours, to check on her again.

She walked back up the hill, toward the stranded, wrecked Falcon. Her first boyfriend had driven one just like it, only his had been brand-new. That same black and white vinyl upholstery: she could practically feel the awful boned strapless bra poking into her rib cage, under her prom dress.

The key to the present stymied Falcon of Desire was in the ignition. She thought she ought to try to back it out of the field now, since the weather was supposed to warm up in the morning and she didn't like the thought of heavy equipment in here, putting down ruts in the slush. She opened the door and got in the car. The floor was littered with Burger King cups and candy wrappers. She turned the key, and a blast of incredibly loud electric music slammed against her. She turned off the radio, put the car in reverse, eased on the gas. The back tires fishtailed, then settled down to a hopeless spin.

Out again on the road, she found what was left of the fence, pulled at it, got some of it straightened out and wound together. She took her keys and left the truck there on the shoulder of the road, to discourage the cows from trying to come out again.

When she had started on the fence, lights were shining from all the windows in D.Z.'s house, but the next time she looked, it was dark down there.

She hoped the girl would be all right.

She turned back toward home, cutting through the meadow where the grove of box elders grew. Now that the wind had laid, the air seemed comfortable, almost warm, sweet-smelling. The snow here was smooth, deep, full of light. She stood without moving, arms by her side, her face raised, the snow falling out of the luminous darkness, through the branches of the box elders. Then, on a whim, she launched herself into a boot-footed jeté across the expanse of snow. And then another.

Whatever you want. Whatever you think would be good for you. Sexy words. She turned on the ball of one foot, danced to no music across the snow with her arms spread behind her. Winged, she was, but not exactly aerodynamic, getting ready to lift off again, all the same, to rise in bulky flight. Her body underneath all her lumpish garments—nightgown and sweater, corduroys and coveralls and parka—felt alive. When she stopped, out of breath, the falling snow in the stillness made little tapping, inquisitive noises against the nylon covering of her jacket. A trickle of melted snow slipped down her back.

Back in her own kitchen, without taking off her jacket or coveralls, she got the broom and swept up the scattering of paper scraps the girl had left behind. Telephone numbers. Jimmy, Bobby Gene, Keith, D.Z.

Poor kid, Jana thought. Poor everybody, wandering around.

She started to throw the litter from the dustpan into the trash, but then took off her gloves and conscientiously picked out the telephone numbers. She didn't know what she was going to do with them, slip them back in the car before the tow truck came, she guessed. Along with a note, maybe—good luck, take care. No, she'd just put them on the dashboard; maybe the girl would find them and maybe she wouldn't.

She set the alarm clock for five, so that she could go down and check on Hera. Before she started taking off her clothes and getting ready to go back to bed, she went once more to look out the window of the back door. She put her forehead against the cold glass, then held her hands on either side to block out the light of the room. All she saw was the snow falling nervously, ceaselessly, out of the high darkness.

"It's all right," she said out loud. Her breath made a foggy shape on the glass—the only ghost she was ever going to see.

But after a minute, she said it again. "It's all right, it'll be all right," she promised. And a picture of the whole farm, with the snow falling over it, over all its ridges and woods and steeps and fields, rose suddenly in her mind.

The World's Room

THE WORLD'S ROOM

Low tide. Somewhere ahead of them the sea heaved out of silence, rested, began again, a long, spent sound, rolling west. Mo walked ahead of her across the wide beach until he was only a narrow shadow on the fog. She bent to pick up a round golden stone. Five lines, like spines, radiated from the center, each with faint crosswise striations.

She put the stone in her pocket and crossed diagonally down toward the sound of the water herself now, walking blind. The small round pebbles slipping against each other under her rubber boots was all that was left of the solid world. The rest was just infinity—mist right up against her eyes, a soft, steady sea wind. Then the foam-edged waves broke at her feet. A flock of herring gulls roosted peacefully out beyond the surf on water that was their same color. They rode its swell and swing.

Ginny turned and walked the water's edge, following the gentle line of the waves in Mo's direction. He was skimming stones. He picked up another, studied its weight, wound up like a pitcher, and threw it as far as he could out to sea. She stood beside him, watching it arc and disappear into the mist. They listened, but couldn't hear it fall.

Then he put his hand on her shoulder. They turned together and walked back up to the top of the beach. Because of the rough sea during the night, the high-tide line was marked with seaweed, plastic bottles, dead fish, tin cans, planks from the lumber ships unloading at the pier in Bell Bay. Lumps of crude oil from the freighter collision two weeks before had caught on the debris. Patches of it lay over the pebbles like tangled black rags.

"Watch what you pick up, Ginny," he said. "If you get that muck on your clothes, you'll never get it off."

They walked east along the high-tide line, picking up planks and pieces of driftwood. When they had as much as they could carry, they crossed the beach and threw the lumber up onto the bank, where they could collect it later, then returned. It was slow work. Ahead of them the long spit of land called the Beak gathered solidity and color. Ginny was in front now, coming to the fisherman's hut. She turned and shouted, "Let's stop now, okay?"

He straightened, holding aloft a red light bulb.

"You look like the Statue of Liberty," she called back to him.

He made his way toward her in long strides. He turned the bulb to one side then the other for her admiration, as though it were a big jewel. "A running light off some ship, probably. It might still work, you know?" He shook it near his ear. "It sounds all right."

"It couldn't possibly have made it up in that surf."

He shrugged his shoulders, raised it up. "But here it is. A safe light, by God. For my darkroom."

"What darkroom?"

"The darkroom that I'm going to set up now that I have a safe light. We'll see if it works." He put it in his pocket, took the wood she was carrying from her. "Now all I need is an enlarger."

"Wait long enough, you'll probably get that, too. A lucky fellow like you."

"Naw, the sea only gives you the signs—you have to get the actual stuff on your own."

They walked up the beach toward the hut. He climbed the wooden steps up the bank ahead of her and threw his armload of wood beside the rutted track, then turned and stretched and looked out toward the sea again, with his hands shoved down into his pockets. He was paying attention now—to what, in all the foggy expanse, she wasn't sure. Paying attention was his calling; his whole body tensed into the act of looking.

Ginny picked her way through the wooden crates scattered beside the hut. She idly upended one under the window on one side of the hut, stepped up on it, and looked in. All she could see at first, peering in the window, was her own reflection against the glass. She blocked the light by cupping her hands around her eyes; still, the only feature of the room was the light coming through the cracks in the boards on the other side of the building, where the lean-to boat shed stood.

But as she looked, some darkness moved across the thin vertical lines of light. She stepped down off the crate, kicked it away from the window, leaned against the wall, feeling like a Peeping Tom. Looking in somebody else's window, what did she think she was doing?

"Good morning," Mo said, out on the track.

There was a metallic clink, then a muffled male voice in reply. Whose? And had he been inside the hut when she pressed her face against the glass? She pulled away from the wall. Roger Simpson, the fisherman, came past the corner then, wheeling his bicycle along the track, back toward the village. He stopped beside Mo. "Beachcombing?"

he asked pleasantly. She cut a glance toward him as he looked her way. His eyes were deep-set, lined, light gray. "Morning," he said to her. She nodded. Maybe he hadn't seen her looking in. His eyes reflected the color of the sky, nothing more.

"Gathering driftwood, actually," Mo answered.

"There's plenty down there," Roger said. He carried his chin at a speculative angle. He was a solidly built man, younger than many of the villagers, though his hair was beginning to gray, curling thickly around his head and down his neck.

Ginny came across the grass toward them, stepping around the crates. She stopped just off the track.

"Most of it's covered in oil," Mo said.

"Bloody tankers," Roger Simpson remarked, with no particular emotion. He ran a square-nailed thumb gently back and forth across his lower lip. "I just thought I'd come out and see if I still had my boats after last night."

They all looked past the hut to the tin-roofed shed that sheltered the two broad-bottomed boats. "They made it through, didn't they?" she surprised herself by asking.

He nodded. His cool gray eyes scanned across her as impersonally as a beacon light, back toward Mo. "Are you here for the autumn then?"

"For the year," Mo answered. His hands were hooked in his back pockets. The two men were almost exactly the same height, and perhaps not too far apart in age—early thirties for Mo, late thirties, probably, for Roger—but Mo's body still carried its boyish ranginess, while the other man, stolid, composed in his white coveralls, looked as if he'd never since the age of about eleven been anything but an adult.

"Oh, well, then." He smiled, his face cracking into deep lines.

"You're in for it." He paused, then continued in his formal voice. "You've taken Mrs. Cleaver's cottage, have you?"

"Yes," Mo answered.

"It's nice and tight."

"I hope so. I'm Moses, by the way. This is Virginia."

Roger Simpson nodded as though they had completed a transaction; it was the way he had nodded when Ginny bought the mackerel from him the evening when she first watched them bring the boats in. He had wiped his hands on a cloth, taken the money from her seriously, counted her change into her hand, then nodded once, his chin cutting down cleanly and finally, as it was doing now. He put his bare hand on the leather bicycle seat. "I must push off or I'll miss my bus to town. I'm pleased you'll be here for a while. Most people just see the place in the summer."

"We'll see it every which way, I reckon," Mo said.

Roger Simpson mounted the ancient bicycle in one long stride, stood the pedals a few strokes, then settled to the seat in an easy forward hunch.

Mo and Ginny turned in the opposite direction. Without speaking, they fell into step together. Pools of water had collected in the ruts; grayish clay coated the feet of their Wellingtons. Mo opened the broken gate in the stone wall before their cottage; it swung on one hinge. They climbed the scooped stone steps and went up the path through the neglected garden, where tall chrysanthemums and roses tangled together, their colors deep in the milky light.

"He wasn't inside the hut, was he?" she finally asked.

He smiled at her. "You Americans certainly are *zealous*," he said, mimicking the saleslady in the shop where they had bought their guidebooks to England's south coast. "Naw. He was just looking at his boats. He came around from the other side."

"God, I wish I hadn't done that."

"It wasn't a big deal—that hut is almost like public property. Forget it."

Inside the cottage, he stood on a chair and took the bulb out of the overhead socket in the bathroom. Then he screwed in the safe light and pulled the chain. The red glow came down on his raised face. He turned and beamed through the eerie darkness at Ginny, who leaned in the doorway. "See?"

"*Now* what will you do?" He didn't answer, busily unscrewing the red bulb and replacing the regular white bulb. "I found a fossil, myself," she told him, shyly. He stepped down off the chair. She took off her work glove and got the stone out of her pocket, handed it to him. "It was a sea urchin, I think." She touched the spokelike lines where the little golden stone lay in the palm of his hand.

He rubbed the impression lightly and attentively. "That's nice, Ginny." He put it back in her hand, looking at her closely with his bloodshot green eyes.

She arranged the fossil on the mantel with the others she had found. Now she put the water on for tea and pulled the rashers of bacon apart while he took the wagon down to the track to collect the wood.

○

They had come to live in this cottage late in August, and now it was the first week of October. The wood was sawed and split and stacked halfway down the drive, though they'd hardly needed a fire yet, except sometimes in the evening. In the garden between them and the sea, summer flowers kept blooming. Perhaps the storm in the night was the beginning of the weather they'd been told to expect, perhaps today the fog would not disperse and leave the blue sky burning above them. But already it was apparent that the storm in the night was an aberration, that this day would by midmorning be like the others in the long, improbable succession, days like beads on a string. "You lead a charmed life," Mr. Clark the grocer had remarked. "It rained all summer long on us ordinary mortals."

Ginny and Mo didn't talk much to each other here. Their charmed life together had taken over, leaving them mainly speechless. Instead, they pointed. At the same moment their arms would go out and there it would be, way off, the pheasant, the fox, the fallow deer. That was how it had been since they came. Miracles like the working safe light had somehow come to them—into their sight, into their hands—at every turn. Miracles were what they had in common.

Because nothing was habitual here, because they weren't moving now to any ordinary logic, but rather to the intimations of accident and suggestion, they took nothing for granted. They moved by signs and omens and lucky breaks. At the very last moment, by talking to someone while they had waited to board the bus that would take them back to their hotel, and then farther west, they had learned about this little cottage, ringed by flowers and the sound of the surf. And now everything seemed miraculous to them, even the ordinary birds at the feeder—the robin, the blue tit, the grackle, who scattered the seed with his clumsy feet. These they watched now, silent, as they sat together at the round table that was the center of their mutual life, drinking their tea from the furnished cups, eating oranges.

They had picked the village by the way it seemed to be situated on the map. They'd left their suitcases at the inn in Black Grange and walked south over the hills, fifteen miles, to find it. It was what they had hoped for, and now, because of a coincidence at the bus stop, they lived here. They planned to stay for a year—that was as far as they had thought. By then they'd be out of money.

Mo sat now with his chair pushed out a little, tilted up on its back legs, one foot in a dirty track shoe propped on the other knee. He was holding the blue cup on his stomach. His face changed, she watched it, as he sank down into his private thoughts. She had only lately noticed how his face would change. In public, it was sociable, alert, open, almost a child's face. The more private he became, the more the face drew toward its center, the place where the close-set eyes met the high broken-looking bridge of his nose, hawklike. He felt her eyes on him—again she felt herself looking in where she had no business to; he focused on her slowly, slowly smiled, set the chair back on the floor, the cup on the table.

She took the spoon out of the blackberry jelly, stood the loaf of rough brown bread cut-side down on the board. "Would you really like to set up a darkroom?" she asked, to talk.

"I've thought about it," he allowed. "I could *use* this place then." He looked up at her quickly. "The painting is so separate—it doesn't have anything to do with this world out here, you know. It comes from somewhere else."

"The city." She had begun to understand how isolated he felt here, though it had been his idea to come this far from London.

He shrugged his shoulders. "From somewhere else. It feeds off—I don't know—other painting. Some kind of razzle-dazzle, I guess."

"Jesus, Mo."

"No," he said quickly. "I like this place. I'm glad we came, I want to stay for a while—it's interesting to me. Only I don't know how to *use* it. Not being a farmer or fisherman myself."

She was perplexed by the idea of needing to use the place—for her, it was enough just to take their walks and look at things. But he was different from her. "You'd do the photography, then, instead of—"

"No. Of course not," he said, with a slight rebuke in his voice. "I'd do both. I'd just go out with the camera when I got too closed in up there with the paints."

She sat nodding, brushing the crumbs around on the table. "Somebody *ought* to photograph this place," she agreed.

"I'd just use it as a way of getting out of myself, making connections. Because otherwise we might both be bouncing off the walls by January."

She carefully pulled out the wilted phlox from the bouquet she had arranged in the jam jar. "*You'll* be bouncing off the walls, maybe."

"Right," he said, grinning at her. "*I'll* be." He stood up and stretched, so that his shirt pulled up from his jeans over his lean, sucked-in belly. "I'm going up to work now. We'll do our walk at eleven or so, okay?"

He went up the steps. For a moment or two the house was absolutely quiet; there was no sound that did not come from the sea, breaking, drawing back, dragging the pebbles with it, breaking again—an ongoing, unmomentous sound, a working sound, like a heartbeat. Then his footsteps began above her, moving decisively up to the canvas, pausing, moving back, over the creaking floorboards. A gull circled the house, screaming out a rusty complaint. Mo turned on the radio. Jagger's voice, like something out of a UFO, a time warp—"But if you try sometime you just might find, you just might find. . . ."

She couldn't get to it, she couldn't hear it right. She needed a translator. She had eighteenth-century ears here. Now the BBC would play Great Moments in British Rock all morning and Mo would move back and forth above her and she would sit in the rose-colored damask chair, choose her pen of the day—red, blue, green, or purple—and open her notebook. In her notebook, in her best handwriting, she would write something. "Least said soonest mended." She saw the trail of green words. "The less said the better.

The less said." And now she folded her legs under her and carefully crossed out the words, blocked them out in precise green rectangles. She couldn't think of any good words. The sea moved, he moved, she sat still in the soft rose-colored chair, looking out the window, then back at the page, which now sprouted flowers amid the green, red, and blue tombstones of deceased words. She turned the page, uncapped the purple pen and wrote: "Come down from there."

○

They went around the coal shed and up the stepping-stone path through the kitchen garden, between Mrs. Cleaver's cabbages and kale. The sun was warm, the haze was gone, the shadows had sharp edges. Sparrows bustled now among the branches of the bay tree, chattering sociably.

They climbed over the back wall and walked up the hedgerow, away from the sea, past the World War II concrete gunner's hut set into the side of the hill. Then they were on the public footpath across the sheep field of Keel Hill Farm. Off in the distance someone was chopping wood; the sound chinked down into the valley.

The footpath passed between Keel Hill House and the confusion of old stone outbuildings in back of it. As they approached, a black sheepherding dog came racketing out of the barn toward them, neck extended.

"Down you," shouted William Gullion, coming out into the doorway of the barn. The dog shifted to a lower key but barked on steadily beside them. William Gullion wore an old black suit with a black waistcoat underneath and a grayish shirt, buttoned right up to the throat. His face was hollowed to the bone and had a polished look, like a stone the weather had worked on. On the other side of the path, in the doorway of the house, a small boy, two or so, stood, naked except for a pair of unbuckled sandals. He studied them with flat blue eyes.

"Morning," William Gullion said, coming toward them, carrying his pitchfork, bowing his head in sober civility. "Just doing a walk, then?"

"Up the ridge," Mo answered. "I hope you don't mind us using the path—where we come from, they'd probably shoot you if they caught you coming across their sheep field."

William Gullion's eyes sharpened slightly toward mirth. "Us only shoots the ones what don't shut gates." He touched the dog with the fork, and it went grumbling, unconvinced, to lie in the doorway of the barn, where it could keep an eye on them. "Bit of weather last night, wa'n't it."

"It took a couple of shingles off down at the cottage," Mo reported.

"You'll see a few more go down, an ye last the winter. Us takes the wind in the teeth out here."

"We won't say we weren't warned, anyhow," Mo answered cheerfully.

"Right in the teeth," William Gullion insisted, smiling grimly over the aptness of the phrase. They all stood nodding and smiling. Finally William Gullion rallied to observe: "Lovely weather now, though. Going straight up the top, are you."

"That's the plan," Mo said.

The child stood transfixed in the doorway, one hand on the doorjamb, the other absent-mindedly clutching his privates.

William Gullion looked back up the ridge. "Old camp's up there, you know."

"We've been wondering," Mo said. "That's where we're headed. We thought it was just a lot of barrows."

"Old camp, from the Iron Age, they say," asserted William Gullion.

"Up in the woods up there is a stone circle as well," he added, a little contentiously, as if to clinch the argument. "Sheep Pen, it's called."

Mo was immediately interested. "Is that right? Can you tell us how to find it?"

William Gullion shifted his pitchfork to his other hand, narrowed his eyes, and nodded vaguely up the hill. "Right up in the woods up there."

"Oh," Mo nodded, breaking into a puzzled grin. "Well, then." He rubbed his hands together and turned to Ginny. "We ought to get going."

Ginny thought of waving good-bye to the boy. She looked over at him. They stared at each other. She decided against it.

They walked up the gently rising fields—they saw no more people. "Do you think he didn't want to tell us?" Mo asked. "Or do you think he didn't know?"

"Maybe he thought he *did* tell us."

They let themselves through stiles, keeping to the edge of the fields where the winter wheat had been sown. Mo had the orange and blue ordinance map stuck in his hip pocket. Often the path disappeared—a hedgerow ran across it, or it had been plowed over. At these junctures, he unfolded his map, figured a way around the hedgerow or field. He stood in his black watch cap, looking up from the map with his quick explorer's eye. She stood waiting, staring back the long way they had come, over the small hedged fields that canted down toward the sea, until he refolded the map and put it in his pocket.

Faithful Indian Guide, Eagle Eye. That's what she called him, when she was trying to explain to herself how it happened that she had gotten on a boat and traveled three thousand miles away from her native land with a man who was still essentially a stranger to her. *He can read maps*, she told herself. He was at home in the world;

he seemed to know where he wanted to go, what he wanted to see when he got there. She thought of him as a kind of navigator—he could tell where he was by a glance at the sun, he knew which way the wind blew. His angular body suggested his grace and eagerness of movement through the world. That's why she had been drawn to him in the first place. She saw herself, in the first months she had known him, sitting beside him in his old blue Scout truck, as he negotiated a maze of back roads, the scenic route to some definite objective—a particular painting in an obscure museum, a stern-wheel ferryboat, a famous Indian mound. He never lost his way.

As for herself, she had sat beside him, her fingernail pressed hard against the thin blue secondary road line on the map, telling herself, *I am here. Now I am right about here.* As a child, she'd been under the impression that west and east were relative, depending on which way she stood, the same as left and right, only farther out. Her natural inclination was still to believe that whichever way she was facing was the north, a basic and deep-seated error of understanding. She wandered through the world now, holding her map upside down when going south, turning the world around to perpetuate the old self-centered illusion that held things together.

But in this place, for the first time in her life, she too knew which way the wind blew—almost always from the southwest. When she turned back the way they'd come, the soft, moist, continuous southwest wind blew into her face. She couldn't remember ever learning anything that had filled her with such an exquisite sense of accomplishment, except perhaps the first word she had ever spelled out and understood—and in fact what she was engaged in here seemed very much like the process of learning to read. And Mo was her teacher.

The world was organized very simply here, as if to help her hang onto her rudimentary sense of direction. Its boundary was the ancient buckled ridge, the highest point of which they were climbing now. The ridge ran in an irregular arc for about fifteen miles. The curve it made echoed the curve of the bay it rose from and returned to, but was somewhat deeper, so that the ridge had the effect of a wall encircling the shallow crescent of hilly fields that lay between it and the bay. This crescent of land must once have been under water, she thought—the ridge had the rugged, embattled look of having stopped a flood; the hills within the arc were, by contrast, gently rounded, as though they had been subdued, ground down to symmetry. The ridge at its height was almost seven hundred feet above the sea, rising and falling erratically, but generally diminishing and finally dwindling to the east into the long spit of the Beak. To the west the ridge met the sea head-on, breaking off as though sliced through, leaving a spectacular golden cliff to face the water.

Between the curve of the water and the curve of the hill lay three small villages, one town, one river, a high road and a low road. Hudstone was east, Bell Bay was west, the water south. A simple geography, limited of course, but complete. This ridge was the edge of the known world. Beyond the ridge lay the great abstraction, the north.

Now they zigzagged in the hot noonday sun up the steep scooped-out face of the ridge at its height. The cultivated fields were all below them; the path wound up around outcroppings of rock through rough fields of gorse, toward the upheaval of old earthworkings at the crest. They crossed the highway and made the last steep ascent to the opening in the western end of the worn circular outer wall of the fortress.

What the fortress had been was still partly decipherable: two concentric walls with a ditch between, an opening in the outer wall to the west and in the inner wall to the north—a primitive maze. The ditch was nothing now but a shallow pit; the walls that once could not have been scaled had recently been grazed by cattle. But the path led to the proper entrance, and they entered there, as the people who had used it would have had to enter, driving their sheep and cattle before them, when the alarm went up—and as the invaders would have had to enter also, if there had been enough of them to storm the gates.

The walls protected an area of about one hundred and fifty yards, full of random depressions. One long platform, about two feet high, rose against the north side of the inner wall, beside the inner entrance. "They probably built a palisade up there," Mo told her. "They'd stand behind it and hold off the enemy with slingshot or something."

He stepped up onto this mound and pulled her up after him. The wind bulked suddenly all around them. They were clear. There was the unimaginable north, fanning out in endless random small fields toward the misty horizon. She turned back toward their village, the solid row of stone cottage fronts curving as the road curved—like a wall, the church tower among the trees. Aldercombe Hill rose sweetly between the village and the sea; Castle Road wound down around it to the washed-out gravel track along the beach. The track ran about two miles, ending beside their own tiny dwelling, Matthew Cottage, on the very edge of the great empty bay. Black-and-white cattle gleamed on the familiar hillsides, shadows of sea clouds raced over the sloping fields. She turned back to face the north. It was like standing on the dividing line between the light and dark of the moon. The white underwing of a hawk flashed in the sun as it cut up into a curve of woods. A river—Mo probably knew its name—snaked along with a pewter glint through a flat flood plain. Hills and streams ran every which way; it seemed an anonymous, haphazard country to her. She knew she'd probably never make any sense of it. She knew her limitations.

But Mo stood beside her with his hands on his hips, looking

around him like a man surveying his own fields, standing where all the other men who had claimed this place had stood—in the same pleased, proprietary attitude, probably—claiming with his eyes what they had claimed in one way or another with their lives. His green eyes were wide open against the wind. This was one more place he gathered into his life but didn't own, didn't want to own, would neither live nor die defending, but claimed, nevertheless, in his own way, as surely as if he'd planted a flag. He turned his head, shaded his eyes, gathered in the details below him.

A sudden, uneasy tenderness surprised her. She put a tentative hand on his arm above his elbow. Underneath her fingers the neat, hard curve of his bicep began. Her hand looked unfamiliar to her against the black wool of his sweater. She thought, almost absent-mindedly, *We're going to die someday, both of us.*

He looked down and smiled at her as if delighted to find her there with him. "Well, here we are," she said into his smile. He put his arms around her to keep her warm. "Here we are," she repeated, her chin on his shoulder. "Not the first and not the last."

"The last for this year, I'll bet—you wouldn't want to be up here in November." He swayed her back and forth in a friendly bear hug.

She stepped back, holding onto her whipping hair. "Don't you wonder who was the first one up here?"

He rocked back on his heels, considering. "Well, I imagine the hunting people had a track along here practically from the beginning. Probably right where the road is. The seaward side of the crest."

She nodded, but after a moment persisted. "But I mean the one who came up here first to, you know, take possession. To stay."

"Oh." He put his mind to it. "It was probably a stronghold for a long time before the Celts fortified it. Probably ever since people first started settling. Some longhead, probably. I guess this is where you'd stake out around here if you were worried about what was coming at you."

She sat down on the mound. "When were the longheads?"

He was pulling on his nylon ski parka. "About five thousand years ago, I think."

"That's not long—what is it, about a hundred and fifty generations?"

He laughed at her. "You figuring on doing a family tree?"

"I was just wondering."

She found her red scarf in her jacket pocket and wrapped it around her head. She raised her arms, turned her head to tie the knot underneath her hair, trying to imagine him. The first one up here. She'd been leafing through *National Geographic*s lately, and remembered a photograph of an aboriginal, his right foot, shod in black fur, propped up in front of him on a boulder. The sharp-edged muscle of his large calf was strained tight as he leaned out, elbow on right-angled knee, over the steep ledge of rock against the fall of the sky. The photograph had been from the side and back, his neck and jaw, but not his face. Not his eyes.

She finished tying her scarf and sat quietly. After a moment, she asked Mo, "Is that why he would have come up here, you think? Out of fear?"

"Or maybe ambition—he might have come up to lord it over what was below him."

"Well, it must have been desperation, one way or the other. Once you were up here, you'd have to keep watching." Mo had moved to the edge of the mound. She watched his jacket snapping and fluttering like a loose sail behind him. "It's a really violent place, isn't it," she said to his back. "Rocks and wind." He wasn't listening, but she went on, after a moment. "He might have climbed up here the same way we did, from the sea."

He looked over his shoulder at her, grinned, and rolled his eyes. "You got *me*, babe—that was before my time." He had the map in his hand. He was getting something straight out to the west. "I think you can see all the way to Exmouth from here," he told her.

She lay back on the mound with her hands behind her head, staring up at the blue sky. She tried to imagine it. How the first man had climbed up here, found it, chosen it. *This is it,* he had decided. *This is where it will have to be.* And then he had gone back and brought the others up, whoever they were, whatever united them in their need to command this view. He dug a pit to shelter in with the woman—there would have been a woman. Together, they lined it with stones. He killed a few deer with his flint-headed spear, sewed the hides together to make a roof: home. He and the others went about their business—a little farming, a little marauding, probably. They smoked the venison, made hoes from the antlers, dug their furrows, sowed their wheat and barley. They did what was necessary to propitiate their gods. And they kept their eyes open. Day and night, through all seasons and all turns of the wind.

He climbed up here, he watched, and then one day he died. His people placed him in a cairn or barrow, his body curled in the fetal position or propped sitting against the wall.

Unless he had not propitiated the gods enough, unless he had stopped watching the one time when he most needed to see, in which case he and his people were probably murdered in their sleep, thrown over the ledge, turned to dust on the wind.

She rose on her elbow, squinted up into the narrow alert face of Moses Hightower, son of an Irish chemist and a German drawer of botanical illustrations, grandson of people he had never mentioned. But then Mo was nobody's son, let alone grandson. The strain of rejection was part of his body's tension, part of its aggressive energy. Somewhere along the line, he had given birth to himself. His face was narrow and sharp when viewed straight on, like a well-crafted, elaborately embellished axhead. And his body was the long spare shaft.

She pulled a blade of grass to chew. "He may be buried—you know, the one who came here first? He may be buried anywhere around here."

"Maybe you're sitting on him."

"Maybe he's still watching," she ventured cautiously.

He glanced down at her, then squatted beside her. "What do you think, Gin? Do you haunt what you remember or what remembers you? How does it go?"

"Well, the land doesn't remember anybody. So it must be the other way around."

"So maybe *we'll* be up here a few thousand years from now, having a look around."

The red bus labored up the hill on its way to Bell Bay, paused at the top, then began its dignified, precarious descent. "We're just transients," she said. "I don't think that counts." Her voice sounded flat in her ears, ungenerous.

"I think sometimes it does." His voice was like a door closing, to protect something, his other places, a curving street in Naples, a rooftop in Paris, Kensington Gardens, maybe, with a girl waiting in a lawn chair. She was just guessing. His places were private. All she knew was that they were all with him, and were his life. "Everyone's just a transient, anyway," he added.

"I don't think you'd feel like a transient if you'd spent your life up here rooting out the gorse to make a field to plant in." His cheekbones seemed to sharpen. They were arguing in earnest about something—whether or not it would be possible for them to haunt this hill fort, apparently. "Maybe some people can know a place better in ten minutes than others do in a lifetime," she said, in awkward conciliation. "Or love it more, anyway. I don't know."

He stayed for a moment more, on his haunches, rocking on his heels. Then he rose thoughtfully, moved off—she watched him walk the walls of the fort in his easy way. He seemed so slight against that other one in her mind, that massive one. He had a runner's body, nothing but spine and legs and breath, stripped down, aerodynamic. Meant to move, not hold his ground.

She lay back and closed her eyes. The sun burned through her eyelids, red blue gold. Her breath seemed frail as dust, yet her ribs rose and fell with her breathing. *My breathing makes me alive; I am alive now. This is my moment in time,* she thought. *We are all transients; history is a river of breath.* She felt herself floating, pleasantly drifting, propelled and supported by the current of her own breathing, in the sun, for her time.

The earth, she thought, falling into a doze, *must be all full of bones by now. Bones of old breathers. It's all right, I guess. . . .* She dreamed a skull. *It's hard to imagine the eyes,* she thought, *when all you have to go on are the sockets.*

Then she was awake. Her senses slipped together, and she was on her feet. Her eyes were wide open. A blue tractor moved far down in a field below the Longacre Farm, turning the black soil for the winter planting, leaving a wake of white gulls roiling in the furrows behind it. Words came to her: *this place at this moment,* and it seemed to her that she could see the life going on below her, at this moment—the men in their checked wool jackets and caps pedaling home from the fields for lunch, the schoolgirls in plaid skirts and green kneesocks walking two by two along the path of yew trees to the dining hall.

But something else was flowing out of the placid blue curve of the water, the round yielding shapes of the hills below, something rose like a flood under the crisp noontide focus, the glossy particularity of the present. All of the people below them, the schoolgirls, the farmers, the district nurse, the grocer, were borne in their particular moments on the current of human time, the continuous accumulation in this one place of human events through unbroken generations.

In her girlhood, she had often seen, looking up from a silent canoe, what the old snake eyes in the swamp saw, the eyes that looked out in the same way at the same thing forever. But it was not eternity that she saw before her here; it was time, it was human feet that she imagined now, moving over this lay of the land, human visions shaping it, changing it, since the beginning of history. *There is no history until there is change.*

And her startled eyes held, for a second, a vision of the changing world. She saw the forests draw back, the cleared land fragment into square hedge-rimmed units. Smoke rose from mud hovels, then from stone farmhouses. Villages formed, went up in flames, formed again. The Romans in well-ordered ranks took this fort in an hour, held it for a century, then were slaughtered themselves. The Saxon farmers carved terraces into the hills; the terraces eroded in time to vague undulations. The monks brought stone blocks in oxcarts up Aldercombe Hill to build the Mariners' Chapel. It rose higher than it was long; its light shone out to sea. The sharp-edged stone of the southwest corner wore into a curve as the wind blew against it for six centuries. In the valley, the monastery was laid waste. The workers' cottages rose, built from the rubble: gargoyles, carved Norman lintels, were incorporated haphazardly into the masonry.

For one moment, watching the blue tractor cutting sharply through the soil, it seemed to her that *she* was the sentry, the ancient watcher, standing hands on hips through weathers and wars for fifty centuries, watching the small cup of land fill up with human designs, watching things change—but not beyond recognition. The black-and-white cattle grazed on for centuries, through wars, invasions, blood, flames, upheaval, chaos. Fields were opened to receive the seed. It had all gone on the same way here, somehow. The grave was dug in the churchyard, the sheep were shorn, their wool lay round their feet. The boats went out to sea, the sea kept its curve, the hills their conformation.

A white Jaguar overtook and passed a delivery van going east on the highway. The Jaguar shifted down, roared past, climbed through the gears again, and her own moment, her own vision, caught up with her. But she knew what she had seen. *Every century is here,* she told herself. Traces of everything that had ever been on this land remained; nothing was wholly lost, not yet, not here, though the electricity pylons stood across the hills from Hudstone to Black Grange like troops amassing at the border.

In the Black Grange Museum, a parish register for 1470 listed a Samuel Batt of this village as a grower of flax. There was a Samuel Batt in the village now—Samuel Batt the butcher, with shrewd black eyes and sanguine complexion. He did not look haunted to her as he packed a few free field mushrooms in with her best end of neck and tied the parcel with white string. But she was haunted, it seemed. She was ingenuous—not accustomed to the proximity of the past and therefore not immune.

She turned and looked around for Mo. He was on his knees on a little promontory outside the eastern end of the fortress. He bent forward, then sat back on his heels, his head cocked to one side. He had collected a pile of oval stones and arranged them in a careful circle, with the largest stones at what she took to be the points of the compass. Now he was fashioning a long arrow coming out of the circle, pointing in the direction of their cottage, slightly east of south. He straightened up, dug into his pocket, brought up a fifty-pence piece, and looked at her. Then he buried the coin in the center of the circle. "You can wish on that if you want to," he said, standing up.

She climbed down off the mound and crossed over to stand beside him. She closed her eyes and wished: to stay in this place until she knew all her directions, until she knew flora, fauna, custom, history, the shape of the seasons. Until she was not a stranger. Then she opened her eyes and looked down at the circle of stones.

"At least," he said, "we won't be gone without a trace."

She put her arms around him quickly. "You wish, too."

"I did. I wished for both of us. That we'd both find what we need to be happy. That we'd both find happiness."

She stepped back from him. His eyes seemed helpless, private, as he looked at her. "Thank you," she said.

He put his arm lightly around her shoulders. "Let's go on home now."

They started down the hill.

"Isn't it strange?" she said. "Every century is here. And now we're here." They crossed the highway and then he went ahead of her down the narrow path.

He was silent for five or ten steps. Then he said, "That's true. Every century but this one."

"Well," she said to his back, "it looks like you can have every century but this one or you can have this one. You get your choice."

"What's yours?" He looked back over his shoulder at her.

She shrugged. "I like it here," she said. She stopped and turned away from him toward the hedgerow. Her fingers moved among the clusters of blackberries; the boughs bent with their heavy bloom.

"I do, too—but it's a doomed world, Ginny. Things are coming at it from fifteen different directions. There's no way it's going to survive the way it's always been—except as a pretty little museum piece."

She stared at the blackberries in her palm. "I don't want to live in a pretty museum piece," she said, in a reasonable voice. "I want to live in my own times. I like penicillin and computers and lasers as much as the next person. But I don't want to give up what's *here*. What's *been* here, all the layers of it."

"It's a National Landmark," he consoled her. He thought she was talking about historical preservation.

They started walking again, single file.

Later, they went through an old iron gate stile that opened onto a series of tiny lush hawthorne-hedged fields, zigzagging down the crease in the hill. In the long deep-green grass of the bottom stood a small stone barn with a slate-tiled roof, shaded by a huge old chestnut tree. She stopped and looked, feeling something for it like an actual pain in her chest. "All the same," she said, "I don't see how you could leave this place. If you were born here, if it were yours."

"If I'd been born here, I would have left," Mo said implacably. "I would have loved it, but by the time I was sixteen, I would have been trying to get the fuck out. To get to where the action was."

"I wouldn't have left," she said, her eyes stinging with tears. "I would have stayed. I would have tried to."

"I know," he said gently. "That's where you and I would have parted company."

○

Elsa Edgeworth, the publican's wife, leaned confidentially toward Ginny across the bar the next evening, settling her collarbones voluptuously in her blue lamb's wool sweater. Elsa did not talk to just anybody. She was drinking white wine, studying the glass as she turned it by the stem, while she told Gin about the new color TV. "An anniversary present. I thought it was terribly sweet of Robin."

"Oh," said Ginny. "Wow." Such a response was clearly not enough to cement this friendship, but she couldn't think what to say.

"I'm counting on it to see me through the winter," said Elsa Edgeworth complacently.

Roger Simpson was standing down the bar from them. Ginny wondered if he had a color TV to see *him* through the winter. She understood that he could hear what they said to each other, if he chose to listen, though he was not facing them. He had turned out into the room, one foot propped up on the rung of a stool. He leaned with his elbows on the stool back, holding his glass of dark ale before him in both hands. The weathered creases around his eyes controlled the repose of his face. Both Ginny and Elsa glanced down the bar toward him at the same moment, then looked back at each other, the tiniest spark of candid speculation passing between them. "It's ever so dreary here once the fog comes down," Elsa continued without missing a beat. "You won't see your shadow for five months."

"That sounds dreary, all right," Ginny allowed.

"You may come to watch the telly with me any evening when I'm not on duty."

"Oh, thanks—that's really thoughtful of you." Ginny saw her reflection in the narrow etched mirror along the back of the bar behind the bottles, with her windblown brown hair, her chapped lips, her healthy, wide-boned, unvarnished American face. *We must be too weird to them even to be interesting.* There she was, like an untidy child in Mo's big brown sweater, looming behind the carefully upthrust, double-knit, strawberry-blonde Elsa Edgeworth.

Elsa raised a small hand, scattering diamond glints among the

Toby jugs hung from the ceiling. "I should be glad of the company. And I expect you'll need some too, poor you, out there in the middle of nowhere."

Roger Simpson turned, his eyes widening wryly as they passed over Ginny's on the way to gesture to Elsa for another of the same.

Elsa stepped down to his glass. "It doesn't feel like the middle of nowhere," Ginny said.

Elsa turned back to her as she worked the draft handle. "Now Roger here loves the winter—he loves all the fog and that." She cocked her head archly at him. "Admit it's true."

"Yes, of course it's true. It's the natural state of things." He reached into the pocket of his gray flannel trousers and pulled out some silver. His hands were articulate—strong-wristed where the cuff was turned neatly back, long-fingered, definite as he sorted through the coins and laid some of them on the bar. His physical presence had the worn, loose ease common to men approaching middle age who had come early to their manhood. He had, it seemed to Ginny, settled down with his flesh. It was as if he'd tested the possibilities of his body thoroughly, as if there were no mystery left, no way it could surprise him, except by giving out on him, and perhaps not that way either. It seemed sad to Ginny, but maybe it wasn't.

"Elsa's not a native, you see," he said, turning politely to Ginny and then back to Elsa. "When you've been here long enough, you'll come to suspect the sun, all those shadows lurkin' about like foreigners." *What an interesting way of putting it*, Ginny thought, and then she thought, *Oh*. He stopped. He put his glass on the bar and turned to her, a blush flowing quickly up his face. "Oh, I am truly sorry," he said. "I wasn't thinking at all. I meant nothing—"

They stared at each other, then she laughed out loud. His face was suffused. He was clearly distressed, but his eyes in a peculiar way stayed calmly out of it, bystanders, almost. "It's all right," she said, feeling a blush rise up her own face. "I don't mind being looked on as a foreigner—it's what I *am*, isn't it." Then she went on, a little wildly, "But I'm going to try really hard from now on not to lurk about."

"Oh please," he murmured.

"Oh Roger, you *have* made a mess of it, I'm afraid," said Elsa, coming in a leisurely way to rescue him. "I see no way out of this at all for you. It's just," she explained to Ginny, "he doesn't think of you as a foreigner, Virginia." He didn't say that that was true. "Anyone who's still here after Bank Holiday is one of us." He and Ginny continued to look at each other for a painful moment, and she saw that his eyes were not exactly calm. They were *locked*, somehow.

Ginny turned and smiled at Elsa. She took a drink from her glass of cider and forced herself to swallow. "I'll be knocking at your door one of these nights when cabin fever sets in, Elsa—we can watch *Coronation Street* or something. I'll even bring my knitting."

Mo was standing by the fire, all in black, with his dark silky hair falling into his face, his lean cheeks sharpened for scholarly attention—he was getting an answer. He turned slightly as Ginny approached, put his hand on her shoulder, and turned back to listen to Penzy Weaver. Sitting against the wall beside Penzy, William Gullion folded his arms against his upright chest, tilted his head, and listened with grave attention to what Penzy was telling Mo, which was that pirate trawlers had fished out the bay the year before.

"They would come by night with no lights," Penzy said. His head quaked slightly as he spoke, a nervous disorder. He flicked an ash toward the tray. Penzy wore a heavy pale-blue fisherman's sweater pulled down over his neatly localized beer belly. The sleeves of the sweater were pushed up above the elbow, exposing his slender white forearms. He had a plump, sad, androgynous face, the spacy abstract eyes of a genius. "The scoundrels ran in so close some nights we could hear the pulse of the engines up here in the village—we had no policing of the bay at all then." His voice was rich, deeply voweled.

William Gullion brought his head down gravely, like a swan, until his chin nearly touched his chest. "It war the Rooshens," he announced to his pint of half bitter half best.

"Or perhaps the French," Penzy gently suggested, glancing up to call Roger Simpson into it, from his post at the bar, where he stood listening.

"I imagine a lot of good English lads were using the drag poles too," Roger Simpson said grimly. "Whoever they were, they took damn near everything. They used nets with small mesh, apparently. They swept the spawning beds clean."

"How long will it be before the bay recovers?" Ginny asked.

"Ah well, the fish are coming back slowly. There's restricted trawling now, and the bay is well policed. But it will never be as it was before. Not in my lifetime, at any rate." Roger leaned against the bar, took up his glass, leveled his gray eyes two inches above her head. He worked in a garage in Hudstone now, she had heard, while he waited for the fish to come back. But sometimes he and his cousins still took the boats out. She had watched them at sunset standing in them, setting the nets, bringing up a dozen mackerel, perhaps a plaice or two.

Now Mo was speaking. This was the first time he had told something, instead of just asking a question and listening to the answer. About the whale, about how, when they walked out of the village on the beach road for the first time to look at Mrs. Cleaver's cottage, the whale had swum beside them all the way. "It has to be two miles out there, you know. If he got too far ahead of us, he'd come circling back like a good dog. It was the damnedest thing."

"Aye, that was the young bottlenose," Roger Simpson said, his face lighting with interest. "I saw him, too, several times, back in August—I can't claim he ever came to heel for me, though," he said, smiling.

"Right, that's when we saw him, the end of August."

"Well, you were lucky."

"They don't come in here," William Gullion mournfully told his glass. "Only the sick ones or the babes what's lost their mums."

Roger Simpson drank off his beer and put the mug down. "Well, I'm off. I promised myself an early night and a clear head. I've got to get home and balance me books."

"Ah, your books is it," said Elsa Edgeworth behind the bar. Roger raised and lowered his eyebrows at her, nodded his sharp finishing nod once all around, and was gone through the heavy oak door. They all looked after him, silently, and drank in silence, and then Mo and Penzy went to play the one-armed bandit, while William Gullion nodded off beside Gin, his back still straight against the wall.

What Mo hadn't told was that, the day when they had walked with the whale, as they reached Matthew Cottage and turned in the gate, the whale had surfaced one more time. They'd seen its smiling bird face quite clearly, turned toward the shore. Then it had headed out to sea. They'd never seen it again; she didn't think anyone had.

She had thought of this occurrence so much as a miracle that it had never occurred to her to wonder what had happened to the little whale. Did it get out? Or did it wash up and die? Or was it still out there in the bay somewhere?

Mo and Ginny left the pub at closing. Now, as they walked back along the narrow street through the village, the smell of woodsmoke filled the clear air; the stars were high and bright. They walked down the hill on the Castle Road, past the tall poplars where the castle used to stand, then home along the sea. They went to bed with the windows and doors open, lay awake listening to the breaking waves, as intimate as breath. The curtains moved in the soft wind, the moon shone in the window.

"It's too pure here," Mo whispered. They lay still, side by side, not touching. She couldn't turn her head to look at him. "It makes me nervous," he continued finally. "It's like living without a clock."

She watched carefully the way the darkness edged across the ceiling as the wind moved the curtains. "I think you ought to go to London this weekend," she said. She felt him turn on his side. "To get whatever you need to set up a darkroom," she added, a moment later.

He had propped his head on his bent arm. His hand traced the contours of her face. "If I go, will you come too?"

"No, I don't think so." She took a breath. "I think you'd better go alone."

She rolled her head on the pillow now to look at him. His body's angles were set by the moonlight as if they were carved in marble. She reached out a hand to his shoulder, half-expecting it to be cool to the touch, but it was warm. His familiar body, bone and muscle, caught in time like her own. His eyes were bright right near the surface.

"Mo?"

"I'd better go tomorrow morning, if I'm going. I'll see if I can pick up some used equipment, then go round the galleries on the weekend. Try to see some stuff I didn't paint myself. I'll come back Monday, okay?"

"Whatever works out—"

○

Friday sunrise. She lay curled under the quilt and watched him buttoning his shirt, worlds away and alone at the foot of the bed. He moved quietly, with a concentrated privacy, around the dim room, collecting a few last things, putting them in his knapsack. She imagined him on that first empty train, being carried along beside the water, then up through the country, Poole, Bournemouth, Southampton, until the city began to gather, and then he would open the door and step out into Waterloo Station, with its vaulted skylit ceilings and its sooty smell of possibility. For a moment she thought she might just throw on some clothes and go with him. She even sat up in bed.

"Don't get up," he whispered, coming toward her. He pressed her head to his stomach. "I'll be thinking about you, baby." She nodded with her face against him, her bare arms tight around his waist.

When he had left she went to stand barefoot, with a blanket around her, at the bedroom window, watching him go down the track through the garden in the pale dawn. He let himself out the gate, climbed the curving track to the crest of the hill, and then he was out of her sight.

She kept standing there, looking at the full moon—it was the harvest moon, she realized, but high, white, remote in the sky now, the world's shining zero. What it all came to and came back to, the same moon, over and over. Under it strode Mo at break of day—up the track with his knapsack to catch the first bus to Hudstone to connect with the first train to London on the cheap return.

The dawn wind was cold. She shut the window, crawled back into bed, pulled the quilt up, and closed her eyes. She tried to think of Mo in London, sleeping on the floor in Chaim's front room off Camden High Street, where she and Mo had stayed together six weeks before, when they had first arrived. In the morning, before he was quite awake, before he had opened his eyes, maybe he would think the sounds of traffic were the sounds of the waves rolling in.

○

On Monday morning, the wind changed around to blow out of the northeast. The kitchen window rattled in its frame; the bay tree in the back garden swayed and turned silver. She wrung the dishcloth and hung it over the edge of the sink. Then she went into the cold bedroom and stripped the bed.

The waves were crashing against the shore; from the window she saw them exploding high into the air beyond the stone wall at the end of the front garden. A thin Monday light settled across the gray-striped mattress.

Now the red mail van came along the track, thirty miles an hour through the gullies. She gathered the laundry and stuffed it into the duffel bag, put on her white canvas coat.

Tom the postman came whistling into the kitchen. "Anybody up?" he shouted. She came out of the bedroom with the duffel bag. His back was turned to her. His black postman's jacket hung in limp, shiny folds, incongruous on his bold shoulders. He set down on the counter the carton of groceries, the pint of milk, the newspaper. "There you are, your every need seen to." He turned to her. *"Almost* your every need, I mean to say." He winked, he grinned. His teeth were strong, flashing white. In a less civilized country he would have been ripping the caps off beer bottles with them. His face was large and horsy and full of pleasant, sociable lust.

"Thanks, Tom," she said dryly.

He had the postcard in his hand. He had, of course, read it. "Lovely picture postcard, that," he said. "I can't help noticing you get lovely picture postcards, not your usual views of Clovelly and the Costa Brava. Now who was the bloke painted that picture? Was that your Rembrandt?"

"Yes. It was."

He smiled, nodding, affecting surprised delight. He'd read that on the back, Ginny thought. She reached out to take the card; he twisted his head to look with her at the portrait of Hendrickje, Rembrandt's patient common-law wife, *Hendrickje Bathing in a Stream*, the light glowing down on her forehead and breast, all draped stately darkness behind her, and the mysterious darkness under her raised shift. *He's not coming back today,* she thought. *Here's the competition.* She unpacked the groceries, put the milk and cheese and butter in the refrigerator.

"This it, Virginia dear?" Tom asked, picking up the duffel bag.

"Thanks, Tom. That's it."

"Vicious wind today, straight from Siberia," he said. "Mind you button up."

"Not the day you'd pick to do your washing, I guess, if you could help it."

"Aw love, we wash on Mondays here, never mind the weather. Mondays, the whole blinkin' country smells like Fairy Flakes."

He took the duffel bag on his shoulder. "Let's go then," he called out heartily, like a conductor, walking ahead of her. She put the postcard in her pocket, unread. She closed the door tight. The gulls were blown white against the gray sky, like scraps of paper taken by wind.

Tom laid the laundry bag beside the white canvas mail sack in the back of the van and settled in beside her. "Mind you take the right sack when you leave, my love. We won't have you launderin' the Royal Mail. Though some of it could use it, I assure you."

"How do you know," she said flatly, for he had read her postcard. He knew her fate—he had not mentioned Mo, had not inquired cheerily whether she was going to let the light of her life back in the house after all his carousing, had not asked if she'd baked a cake.

"Why do you think we postmen have our kettles and camp stoves, eh," he asked, unfazed. "Steam 'em open. A little human interest along with our tea."

She stared ahead of her through the salt spray that collected on the windshield like rain. She sat with Rembrandt against her thigh and saw

Mo headed for the National Gallery, right from Waterloo Station, saw him crossing the bridge, passing in a hurry up toward the Strand, his knapsack on his back, threading through the sitters in Trafalgar Square. She saw him take the gold-framed glasses from their case, duck his head to slide the glasses on. He folded his arms across his chest; he stood for a long time before the painting *Hendrickje Bathing in the Stream*. Later, in a shop somewhere near Soho, he would kneel to examine a second-hand enlarger. Lovingly, he would test its movable parts.

She wondered what images he would enlarge with it.

She took the card from her pocket, turned it over deliberately, made herself read it, bumping along in the bucket seat beside Tom. It had been posted on Saturday. It was written in pencil in his hurried round script. "Dear Ginny," it said. "There's a show opening Tuesday that I really want to see, so I'll be back Wednesday. Wednesday for sure. Here's what I'd show you if you were here. Wish you were here. Love, Mo."

Tom looked at her. "Bad news?" he inquired solicitously.

She shot him an evil glance. "We'll just have to wait till the next postcard, won't we," she said. "Then we'll know."

○

Delphiniums bloomed against the gray stone wall of the back garden of Mrs. Cleaver's house in the village. The fat yellow lab slept in front of the fire. Armloads of flowers—dahlias, snapdragons, daisies—had been set in copper basins in the wide white windowsills. A lorry squeezed through the medieval street, its side passing inches from the window, causing a momentary eclipse—the flowers darkened, then the light seeped over them again. In the kitchen, Ginny's laundry was hoisted to the ceiling on the airing rack, drying in the heat that rose from the Rankin range.

Ginny and Mrs. Cleaver sat on opposite sides of the fire, Mrs. Cleaver in her blue jersey dress and brown beads and nylon stockings, Ginny in a white turtleneck sweater and jeans and Red Wing boots. Ginny held a photograph in a silver frame in her lap, a photograph of two men. One was slight, with the blond, wizened good looks of an aging ex-child actor—theatrical eyebrows, small, square smile, rakish stance. His hand was on the shoulder of a taller man, who had a dark mustache and white hair, black eyes in a smooth, tanned face. The taller man smiled quizzically at his companion. They were a droll pair, like a successful vaudeville team: the Honorable Alan, who had been the village's landlord, and Mrs. Cleaver's husband, Julian.

Mrs. Cleaver cocked her head to look across at it. "My son Michael—the one on the farm near Blandford now—took that picture. Four years ago, it is now." She leaned forward to brush imaginary crumbs off her lap, then said suddenly, as if giving in to an impulse she didn't like the look of: "The film came back from Black Grange the day after Honorable Alan's funeral. We had it blown up and framed as a sort of memorial, not knowing my Julian would be dead the same month of the next year." She took a sharp breath, looked up from her lap at Gin, and went on in her rough, straightforward voice: "I can't reconcile myself." She rested her head against the back of the chair. The veined lids closed over her black eyes, then opened again. "If only Honorable Alan had not died first, everything would have stayed just as it was."

Ginny stood the photograph back on the oak table between them, and Mrs. Cleaver took up her knitting once more. The wool flowed through her fingers; she composed her face to concentrate on counting the precise crimson stitches as they moved swiftly down the silver needle toward the busy points. After a time, she went on. "But he did die, of course. For no good reason—drink killed him, an accident. He fell down that flight of stone steps at four o'clock one morning after a full night of it." She laid the baby sleeve she was knitting in her lap. "He was a shocking rake, but no one can say he wasn't a good landlord. He stayed here most of the year, you see—he really lived here, unlike most of them, and looked after things. He only went up to London at the weekends." She smoothed the sleeve caressingly, cocking her head. "Stone, they were," she finished vaguely. "The steps. He was dead before he finished falling, broke his neck. A waste, that's all it was. He wasn't yet fifty. A waste and a shame and a terrible pity—for all the village, not just for us."

She shook her head sharply and looked up. "For then, you see, the estate passed to a nephew who has extensive holdings up in the North. He's not much interested in this poky little place. He put it right into the hands of an estate agent in London. And we were the first to know what that meant."

Ginny already knew what it meant—they'd lost the lease on the farm. The day she and Mo had come to inquire about Matthew Cottage, Mrs. Cleaver had brought them to sit in the garden and had mentioned, with a negligent wave of the hand, "That was all our farm; that was all Mariners' Farm. It went straight up Aldercombe Hill and all the way down to the sea."

Now Mrs. Cleaver sat with her shiny blue-veined hands clasped over her knitting. In back of her, through the French doors, beyond the garden, the Mariners' Chapel stood golden under the gray sky, at the top of the hill. The sea was visible between one hill and the next. To lose that—

"I'm sorry," Ginny said helplessly. She reached across to put her hand on Mrs. Cleaver's. "I'm so sorry this has happened to you."

"Well," Mrs. Cleaver said, patting Gin's hand, "what can't be changed must be accepted. And yet I can't seem to accept it. It was our life and what we meant to pass on—we always assumed. Just assumed, you know, because that was the way it always had been—"

Her voice trailed off, and they sat in their opposite chairs, staring at the small fire. "Before my dear was in the ground," she said, pounding the arm of the chair with her fist, "they were come from London to say the sons could not take up the fathers' leases on the farms anymore. There was Julian Cleaver in his coffin in the church, and the estate agent at the door. We thought he was come to help us through, as Honorable Alan would have done. He sat down in the chair where you're sitting now, he even took some port, and then he told us that all the farm land in the village must go back into the control of the estate as it fell vacant. But I might stay in the house. Michael took him out of his chair, I'm afraid. Michael set him down outside the door. The agent got into his car and hightailed it back to London, and we went over the road for the funeral.

"There was I, kneeling for prayers at my dear one's grave, and not even praying—calculating, I was. I hardly heard the words of the sermon, I was so busy doing sums in my head. I know he will forgive me for it." She fingered her pansy-bordered handkerchief and pressed it efficiently to her nose. "We owned our stock and machinery, anyhow, and we had our savings and the refund of the balance of the lease money, and that evening I said, 'Never mind, Michael, you shall have a farm, and a good farm, too, and freehold.' Two months later he was building his bungalow on the land we'd found up near Blandford.

"By then our farm was being offered to the other farmers in the village on short-term lease. All of them went together to say they would never touch it at all, and for three years it lay vacant. Just now someone from Little Knowle has taken it by the year to run sheep on. And still no one knows why the estate must have the land back. A new rumor starts every week, but it's all guesses. Some say they're trying to give the whole village to the National Trust—next time you see us, we'll be standing outside the Manor House taking up tickets, eh? Some say they want to consolidate the farms and run them as one big operation for efficiency, but no one knows anything.

"My own feeling is that they're going to build retirement bungalows down near the sea and lease them to wealthy folk from the Midlands. What we'll have here is a picturesque retirement village. And perhaps that won't be a bad thing. All these run-down cottages in the village will be renovated as they fall vacant. In three years, the pub will be full of old duffers every night. We'll have enough in tithes to repair the church steeple. The butcher will get rich. You'll see." She remembered her knitting, took it up again, and settled over it comfortably. Then she said in her breathless, brusque voice, "No you won't, dear. You'll be long gone, I forgot. In three years you'll be two years gone." She took in a sharp gasp of air to change the subject, nodded at the biscuit tray. "And how is Moses Hightower, that beauty?"

Ginny placed a custard cream carefully on her saucer. "He's up in London for a few days."

"I expect he's getting a bit restless," said Mrs. Cleaver matter-of-factly, leaning forward to throw a few more sticks on the fire.

○

Ginny walked back home on the track in the late afternoon, her duffel bag of clean, folded laundry slung over her shoulder. The wind blew straight out of the hills; she climbed down the bank to shelter from it.

The beach was an empty gold expanse. She and the gulls and the sandpipers had it to themselves. Three big ships—tankers probably—moved like bulky ghosts along the horizon in the shipping lanes. Within the bay the waves broke and broke, rolling in at a slant across the metallic curve.

A single gull wandered in her direction at the last reach of the breaking waves, like an aimless old beachcomber. She noticed it because, as the distance between them shortened, the gull didn't take flight. It minced forward, up the strand toward her, with a bright blank eye—like an old boy rolling home.

Then she saw its stained, disheveled plumage. She moved irrationally away from it, cutting a wide circle around it. It wandered on past her toward its particular hawk or fox or slow starvation, still leading with its jaunty military breast. She knew what you were supposed to do when you saw them like that. But she didn't think she could do it. *It would turn out not to be a mercy killing*, she told herself. She walked on a few steps, the bird's fate flowing all in back of her. Then she stopped. If she couldn't kill it, she had to save it. She had at least to try. She put the duffel bag down under the bank, took off her coat, wet with sea spray, and turned back.

The bird had stopped and turned to the sea, as if to contemplate the horizon. She walked quietly behind it, holding her coat on her arm, but before she was close enough it sensed her, hurried toward the water, spreading its ragged wings, actually lifting itself in a desperate commotion a foot off the ground. It came down again, bustled silently away from her, pumping its wings awkwardly to try again, to keep on trying. But she had her coat quickly over it and scooped it off the ground. One black-tipped wing escaped, extended itself, wildly beating up into her face. She pinned the bird against her side with one arm, got the free wing down with her other hand as the gull struggled silently under the coat.

It was solider than she had expected it to be, like a medium-sized cat. The claws flexed helplessly within the folds of thick material. She felt along the gull's shape to find its head and worked the coat open to give it air, then came across the beach walking fast toward the fisherman's hut, where she could get up the bank using the steps. Her cheek stung where the wing had grazed it. She pressed the gull close against her, inside the wet coat. Her sweater had dampened with spray, collecting the cold.

The bird didn't struggle now. She felt its absolute, concentrated stillness. "It's all right, don't worry," she crooned, as she climbed the steep steps. Picking through the fish crates, she came out on the track now, and Roger Simpson was standing before her, in a dark blue sweater, with his dirty white mechanic's coveralls zipped over. "Come along inside here and let's see what you've got hold of," he said.

"A herring gull," she told him. He went slightly ahead of her, his head bowed.

"Oil?"

"Yes."

"I saw you stalking it. I imagined that's what it was."

He opened the door and she stepped past him into the dark room that smelled of old rubber and damp wood. "It's grazed your face," he remarked. He closed the door. The wind whistled through the cracks. He lit a paraffin lamp and hung it overhead on a hook, then looked at her in the wavering light, in a distant professional way, and turned to a shelf, where he rummaged for a moment among a clutter of bottles and rusted equipment. "It's a shambles in here," he remarked, with his back to her. "Well, that's what happens."

She stood where she had stopped, clutching the gull, in front of a table on which had been piled cork floats, twine, knives, rusty weights, chains. Nets, oilskins, odd clothes hung from nails along the walls. A dozen oars leaned in the corner behind the door. The room's only furnishings were the table, a cot against one wall on which more fish crates were stacked, a coal stove on the opposite wall, a chair with the back broken out of it.

He came back now with two bottles. He set them down and cleared a space on the table. She held onto the gull with both hands. He uncovered the head carefully, rolled the coat down a little way. The gull made a small sound, high-pitched, like a frightened supplication. Then it was silent. Roger Simpson closed one hand gently and slowly round the bird's neck and ran his fingernail into the heavy, begrimed plumage of its mantle. She saw that the down underneath was still white and soft. The bird stayed still under her hands, regarding Roger Simpson with its yellow, waiting eye.

"Usually they don't pull through. It will have swallowed a lot of oil trying to preen," he told her. "It might be kindest to go ahead and wring its neck. I'll do it for you, if that's what you want."

"No—I want to give it a chance. I'll take care of it. If it lives a few days, it might pull through."

"So might we all," he said, smiling toward her briefly. "Well, we'll do what we can for it." He shoved the bottles forward one at a time on the table. "This one's for you. This one's for the gull." He fished a folded handkerchief out of his pocket and uncorked the brown bottle. "Iodine," he said—and dipped the handkerchief into it. "Turn your face," he instructed clinically, wiping lightly down her cheek. "It's just a scrape," he said then, as the burning started. "But you look a bit messy—there's no water here, I'm afraid." He studied her quietly as he put the top back on the iodine. "You're cold," he announced.

He sorted through the garments hanging on the nails and took down a black wool jacket. He draped it around her shoulders as she stood with her hands on the gull, then picked up the other bottle. "Mineral spirits," he said. "You'll want to clean just about an inch downward a day—too much dries out their skin. We'll do the face and claws now." The gull watched the man, as he wet another part of the same handkerchief.

"It doesn't look afraid of you," she said.

He laughed. "It never learned to look afraid—it only learned to fly away." Its head moved sideways within the collar of Roger Simpson's hand, as he began now to clean the face. He worked in a meticulous, unhurried way around the yellow beak with its bright red dot like a spot of fresh blood.

"If you'll just lift it for a moment, I can get at its claws. That's it." She picked up the gull awkwardly. It felt like a swaddled baby. He uncovered the feet, embedded with oil. He took hold of one of them with a firm movement, pressing it out to clean each claw and then the webbed skin between. The claws of the other foot flexed and curved arthritically, helplessly. He bent around to keep his shadow off the bird. He worked methodically, silently, then straightened. "All right. You can let loose now."

She put the gull on the floor and took her coat away. The bird hunched there for a moment, low to the ground, broken-looking. Then it ruffled its sticky plumage, organized itself, and scuttled quickly under the cot.

He put the top on the mineral spirits. "Can you take this on?"

"I already have. But I don't know what I'm supposed to do. How long do I have to keep it?"

"Till it molts—a month or so, I expect."

"I'll build it a pen out in the back garden."

"You can leave it here if it comes to that," he said, offhandedly. "If you don't mind the trouble of walking down to feed it every day. You can just spread newspapers. As you can see, there's nothing much to bother."

"You're sure? It wouldn't be any trouble for *me*. I generally pass this way once or twice a day anyway."

"You and your husband are serious walkers, aren't you." He

smiled a one-cornered smile. "We're a little disappointed, actually—you're our first Americans. We thought you'd have a motorcycle, at the very least."

"I suppose we're just your luck."

"Yes. I suppose you are." He continued to smile, and she felt as though she were looking into the shining, straightforward gaze of a blind man. She thought of explaining about the *husband* part, but she couldn't think how to do it. She had no doubt that Roger Simpson was someone's husband—he wore no wedding band, but he had a solid, settled, long-married look.

"Well, I *will* leave it then. If you're sure—"

"Yes, of course," he said. "Don't give it a thought."

"Thank you." They nodded at one another.

"I'm afraid you've ruint your coat."

She glanced down at the white canvas, smeared with oil and bird droppings. "Oh, well," she said vaguely, rolling it absent-mindedly into a bundle. "Maybe I can wash it. What do you feed it?"

"Nothing fancy. It's a scavenger, you know. It wouldn't turn down a herring, but these boys can make do on anything—garbage, sewage, carrion."

"Survival of the least particular."

"Can't hold that against them."

She pulled the musty old wool coat together at her throat. Her eyes moved over his windburned face, the curlicued red embroidery spelling out his name on the pocket of his coveralls. "No. I don't."

He put the bottles back on the shelf. "The easiest thing would be to buy a half-dozen or so tins of cat food—something with a fish base—and leave them here, with a can opener and a spoon. A small tin a day ought to do."

"All right."

They were both silent for a moment, listening to the wind blowing up around the hut.

"Why did you and your husband choose this place?" he asked suddenly. "I assume you could have gone anywhere in the world."

"Mo's not my husband." *There*, she thought, and made herself look straight at him. "He's"—she raised and dropped her hands, baffled—"a friend. A good friend."

"Oh," he said. "Pardon me—I didn't know. One takes it so for granted around here, the married state."

"It's all right. It just feels wrong to let people go on assuming. . . ." Her voice trailed off. "Anyway, I guess it's true—we *could* have gone anywhere in the world. I wanted to come to England, and Mo's lived in London a few times and remembered this part of the coast. So we studied our maps and guidebooks and chose this village. If we hadn't liked it when we actually saw it, I guess we would have gone on farther west. But we liked it. So we stayed."

He looked at her as she gave this explanation, wrinkling his brow in comic incredulity. "Do you know how strange that sounds?" He gave a little bark of surprised laughter. "It's right reassuring, though, when you come to think of it—I mean, for the ones of us who didn't get here by studying a map. It makes me think I'm living bang at the center of the universe."

She smiled and shrugged her shoulders, feeling foolish.

"And—you're satisfied here?"

"Yes," she said. She wanted to say more; instead, she said, "Yes," again, more definitely, nodding. He nodded back, looking at her intently, his long lips set gently together. "And you?" she asked cautiously. "Do you like it here?"

He gathered himself. "Ah well," he said, in deprecation, "I've lived here all me life."

"That's why I ask—do you still like it here? In spite of—everything?"

"Well, things change, don't they. That's the way of things. Nothing keeps."

"This world kept for a long time."

"Yes," he said flatly. "But now it's changing, inn'it."

They both looked up now as the rain came suddenly in sheets across the tin roof, intensifying, diminishing.

"We must find something for that poor creature to eat," he said. "We used to keep some tins of things around—" He looked hopelessly at the shelves.

"Oh, I know—Mrs. Cleaver wrapped me up some sandwiches to bring back—they'd do, wouldn't they? Oh! My laundry," she remembered in dismay. "I left it on the beach. It'll be soaked."

"Shall I go?" he asked quickly.

"Oh no, I'll go."

"I'll go," he said. "Where is it?"

"It's in a duffel bag. Under the bank, down the beach."

He was putting a black oilskin on over the coveralls, pulling on his Wellingtons. He took a rain hat from a nail and tied it under his chin. She looked at him, mesmerized. He smiled and raised his eyebrows. "Quite the old salt, eh."

"You look like you came off some old clipper ship or something," she said.

"No doubt I did," he laughed.

When he had gone out the door, she put her arms through the sleeves of the coat that was still hanging around her shoulders and buttoned it over her damp sweater. Then she went to kneel under the cot to check on the gull. But she could only see its huddled shape in the dark far corner.

She found a coffee mug and set it outside to fill under the dripping roof. She saw Roger Simpson walking down the beach, head lowered against the rain, the black oilskin twisting around him in the wind. When the cup was full, she took it back inside and placed it on the floor beside the cot. Maybe they drank salt water. She'd have to find out. Or leave one of each. She found some old *Daily Telegraph*s in one of the crates and spread them carefully over the dirty floor, moving paint cans and odd buckets and boots to the corners of the room. The darkness had thickened, the yellow light from the lamp concentrated in a pool over the table. She went to stand at the window. The rain ran now in thick sheets down the glass.

An old photograph was propped on a shelf beneath. She picked it up and held it to the weak light that come through the window. Quite a day for images—first Hendrickje, then the Honorable Alan and Julian Cleaver, and now the astonishing young Roger Simpson. He stood in a Naval uniform on the deck of a ship of some sort, leaning against a rail, legs crossed, hands in his pockets, laughing (joyfully! she thought), all white teeth, up into the camera.

The sudden draft behind her made the newspapers rise and settle, and then the door closed. She glanced at him over her shoulder as he settled her duffel bag on the backless chair. She looked back at the photograph, then put it down, and turned back to him. "You were in the Navy?"

"Oh yeah. They tried to make me into an officer," he said. He gave a small head-shaking smile. "I told them all I wanted was to come back home and fish. It was their opinion that I had no ambition. They were right, I suppose. The first night I was back in England, I took the late train to Hudstone. From there I walked home along the sea. When I reached the hut, it was three in the morning. I fell asleep on that cot over there." She turned her head to contemplate it. "My mates found me here, still in my uniform, when they came at dawn. They woke me and we took the boats out. The pilchards were running in a great silver roil. I'll never forget it. I felt they'd laid it on especially for me."

He was standing with his hands still on the duffel bag. "Why do you stay here?" she asked. "If it's as you said, if it will never be the same out there?"

He gave a short laugh. "I'm a person who stays." They stared at each other for a moment, with the rain slipping over the roof and the water dripping down his face. "Do you think me a fool?"

She felt so deep in that question that she might live and die there. "No," she answered, finally. She came across the room, hesitated, then took the duffel bag from him, unclasped it, pulled out from the damp clothes the sandwiches wrapped in waxed paper, tore the soft bread into pieces, and arranged them on the floor. They waited. There was a tentative rustling under the cot, but the gull didn't come out of its hiding place.

"It won't come out while we're here," he said. "I'll get what I came for and be off." He picked up a tarp in the corner and folded it over his arm. "You'd better take one of these oilskins. And don't forget your coat." He rolled it in newspapers and stuffed it into the top of the duffel bag.

She took an oilskin from a peg and put it on self-consciously over the wool coat he had given her earlier. "I'll bring these back tomorrow," she said.

"And a hat, too," he said seriously, holding one out to her, which she took and obediently tied under her chin.

"Now you're just off the clipper ship, too," he said.

He extinguished the lamp and held the door for her. She picked up her duffel bag and walked out ahead of him into the sheeting rain. "I'll leave this key with you. I've another at home." He locked the door and dropped the heavy old-fashioned iron key into her hand.

He took hold of the handles of the bicycle and rolled it out onto the track. He stopped and looked in her direction once again, through the rain. "Well, Virginia."

She nodded, amazed that he remembered her name.

"I expect that gull is glad you picked out this place on the map."

"I hope he likes Mrs. Cleaver's lobster paste. Thanks for showing me how to take care of him—I probably would have put him in the dishpan and tried to scrub him down."

He smiled. "That would have solved your problem, anyway." He gave a wave and was off on his bicycle, the wind at his back.

She shouldered the duffel bag. The light had gone to purple; the rain blew in her face. The sound of the wind and the sound of the waves twisted together into the same sound, the only sound. She climbed the track to the top of the hill, looked down on Matthew Cottage, and saw, through the gusts of rain, two squares of yellow light.

○

She walked down the hill, lowering her head to the rain, and turned in through the broken garden gate. The flowers thrashed in the wind. She went up the path toward the front door, and through the window saw Mo sitting in the pink damask chair, in his old Army jacket, his long legs stretched out before him, his elbows on the arms of the chair, his hands laced over his stomach. Another photograph, he seemed, caught in that unexpected square of light, framed by the window. She came into the house and closed the door behind her.

He turned his head, studied her smilingly for a moment. "Surprise," he said.

She unhitched the duffel bag from her shoulder and set it down. "You've built a fire," she said. Water dripped off around her onto the rug.

"We needed one, for sure," he said. She went into the kitchen and took off the oilskin and the old black coat and hung them on a hook. The enlarger was on the kitchen counter, gray and imposing, like a big laboratory microscope. She came back into the front room and stood untying the rain hat, looking down at him, but he offered no explanations, just looked back at her, smiling. She turned her back to him, holding her hands out to the fire. Her sweater smelled doggy as the damp wool warmed.

"I'd better change my clothes," she said finally.

"I turned the bathroom heater on for you," he said, from his sprawled position.

"Oh, thanks. I'll have a bath then. I'm chilled all the way through."

"I figured you'd be a little bedraggled if you had to walk back in this. I didn't think you'd be mauled though."

"Oh! I forgot about that. I'll tell you all about it later. Did you get caught, too?"

"No, I got back a little before it began." They smiled at one another again, everything held in puzzled reserve. Then he looked back at the fire.

She knelt in the dark to turn on the hot water faucet. The gas hissed up in the Astor water heater through fifty tiny jets. She counted to eight and finally the flame erupted, yellow and blue. She adjusted the flow of water until only the blue part of every separate flame remained. Then she looked at herself in the mirror over the sink, in the light slanting in from the hall. She reminded herself of a bear surprised in a cave—her wet hair hung dark and heavy around her shoulders. Her cheek was streaked with iodine and dried blood. Her lips were chapped to a deep red. Her eyes stared at her, dark and startled, from someplace far back. She undressed and slid down into the long narrow tub of hot water, lay back. Her legs didn't reach the other end—they floated out in front of her. Her toes broke the surface.

She sat up and filled her hands with water, lifting them up to her face over and over, shampooed the salt out of her hair, then lay back again under the warm water for one minute, encased by the narrow sides of the tub in a kind of stillness, blankness, peace, like the peace between waves. Then she forced herself up out of it. She let the water out of the tub, slipped on her flannel robe, combed her wet hair, put antiseptic cream on her cheek. She hung her wet sweater and jeans on the rack to dry, turned off the heater, went back into the front room.

He was leafing in an aimless way through the magazine section of *The Observer* and looked up as she entered the room. She sat on the floor beside the fire, barefoot, combing her wet hair. He dropped the magazine beside the chair. The rain beat against the window.

"Your postcard came today. I'd planned to meet your bus when I finished doing the laundry at Mrs. Cleaver's. But since you weren't coming, I just came on back." She glanced at him. He was watching her the way you'd look at someone you were painting, eyes narrowed a little. "Are you hungry? I baked a chicken this morning for us to have tonight—back when I still thought you were coming. I'm a little confused."

He smiled. "Let's just sit here awhile. It's nice, here by the fire."

She leaned back against the arm of his chair, closed her eyes, felt the comfort of the fire beginning to touch her under the skin. "On my way back," she said drowsily, "I had to rescue a gull. It had gotten into the oil."

"What did you do with it?"

"Roger Simpson was there at the hut. He said I could keep it there. He told me how to clean it and what to feed it. You must have passed by while I was in there."

"You think it will live?"

"I don't know."

"That goddamn oil." After a moment he asked, "How long do you have to keep it?"

"Till it molts, he says. A month or so."

He nodded, reached out and took the comb from her, and combed her hair. "Do we have any wine?" he asked, finally.

"Only the sherry."

He got up and poured two glasses, brought them back to the fire.

"You're like a stranger here," she declared suddenly. "Like a guest. Because I'd given up on you. And now here you are."

He looked down at her for a moment, then stooped to kiss the top of her head. He handed her a glass and sat down again.

"How odd," she said in a low voice.

"Odd?"

"That you should be sitting in just that chair, out of all the chairs in the world."

"Mrs. Cleaver's chair, soft as a grandma's lap? You don't think this chair and I have been headed for each other from the beginning?"

"It could have been any chair, anywhere. It's pure chance."

"Does that frighten you?"

"Yes."

He turned the glass rim against his lips. "Chaim is going to Johannesburg for several months. He asked if we'd like to have his flat while he's gone. For the rent he pays—something ridiculous, thirty pounds a week, I think."

She lowered her head to the glass and sipped the fumy cheap sherry. "That's why you came back this afternoon after all?"

"Yes—to put it on the table, the idea of having both places. He's leaving Friday. Ten other people want it, of course. He's given us first refusal." He paused. "And I thought we ought to talk about it."

"I think we ought to take it, Mo," she said, holding her glass up and looking at the fire through it.

"You do?" As though he had not dared hope.

"Are you kidding? It's really good luck. Of course I think so."

"And then we'll have a city house and a country house?"

"Just like Elizabeth and Philip."

"It'll cut a few months off how long we can stay, you know."

"Well—maybe something will happen. Maybe you'll sell a painting or something. I'll have to stay here, mostly, for the next month, to take care of that gull, if it pulls through. But after that I'll come to visit there. And you'll come to visit here." She stopped short. They glanced at each other with courteous stunned eyes, then away. "I didn't know that's what I meant," she said, looking down at her hands, turning her turquoise and silver ring from New Mexico on her finger. "But that's how it'll work, you know—that will be your place and this will be mine, and we'll visit each other." She heard her voice going on evenly, reasonably. "I'll cook for you; we'll take our walks and explore everything. If it isn't raining, we'll go to the pub at night. And I'll come up there sometimes, and we'll go to a movie and to the Indian restaurant afterward. Or to the Tate. What could be better?"

He touched her cheek. "The gull did that?" She nodded. He brushed it thoughtfully for a moment. "Let's see this baked chicken you're trying to seduce me with."

"And a pie," she said seriously. "Blackberry pie, the last one this season."

It was all settled. The rest of the night was in the nature of a celebration. Hilarity set in. They drank the whole bottle of sherry. They treated each other with playful broad gestures. They built up the fire and lay before it, they rolled around on the floor laughing, clutching their stomachs helplessly, tears sliding down their faces. They sat at the table, pushing the dirty dishes aside, and made their budget, their projections, their plans. He knew where he could sell a painting for a couple of hundred pounds; he was going to write to his brother and ask him to sell the Scout truck. She could get some money from home. They could stay the year, they could even stay longer, they could have their cake and eat it. They threw down their pencils victoriously. It was so easy it was like a dream.

And, seriously now, everything considered—what they were, what they each needed—what *could* be better? *I will visit you and you will visit me and nothing will be lost.* He put his arms around her and swayed her in her flannel bathrobe to the hokey '40's music on the BBC. When the rain stopped, she pulled on her jeans and boots, and they walked out on the wet shining beach to the water's edge, where the dark sea rose and broke and drew back before them.

"When you come up to London," Mo said, "I'll show you a good time, baby. I'll show you—the sights. I'll go around collecting sights to show you when you come up."

And it was all settled. He had to go back on Thursday with a check for Chaim. He would take back his paints and tools and set up a little studio there. "I'll leave the darkroom stuff here. That's what I'll do when I'm here—print." He would be back again on Sunday, to bring the chemicals he needed, and to pack things.

At dawn, she folded the oilskin and the wool coat over her arm, stuck the black rain hat on her head, and took the iron key off its nail. Mo came out into the hallway, pulling his sweater over his head, raking his hair out of his eyes. She held up the key. "Now," she said, "I'll show *you* the sights."

○

The key turned the heavy bolt. She stepped ahead of him into the dim room. She stood aside for him to come in behind her. "Jesus," he said. "Chaos."

"Oh! It ate the sandwiches!"

"Where is it?"

"Under the cot, I guess." He knelt to look.

She hung the coat and oilskin carefully on their hooks, took off the hat and set it on a shelf with the others. "Is it dead?"

Mo opened the tin of sardines they'd brought with them, threw one under. They heard the immediate rustle as the gull moved to it. Mo placed another at the edge of the cot. They waited, keeping quiet. The gull stretched its head out, nipped the sardine up in its beak and held it there, as if trying to call up from somewhere the forgotten processes of hunger, then had it down in one gulp. It came out from under the cot, frantic and serious, wings extended, yellow bill snapping, catching the sardines as Mo threw them. "Mighty hunter," he said.

She uncapped the mineral spirits. She put on her leather gloves. He took the towel they'd brought along for holding the gull. "I'd better see if I can manage it by myself," she said, apologetically. He handed her the towel and stepped back. She threw the towel around the gull, quickly pinned it between her knees, and held it by the ruff around its neck, close up, so that it could not duck its head and peck her. Mo set the bottle of mineral spirits beside her, then leaned against the wall, watching her. "Leda and the swan," he remarked. "Only upside down."

They were both subdued, self-conscious. It was Roger Simpson's place.

Also, it was Roger Simpson's gull. She had only found it. She felt he was letting her take care of it. She thought of the expert way his hands had moved on it, as though he'd done that job many times before. It was much more difficult, trying to hold the gull with one hand, work on it with the mineral spirits with the other. But she did the best she could, rubbing carefully down the inside of the neck and around behind the head, above the wings. It did not struggle, pressed between her knees. But she felt its alertness, how it was poised for its first chance. She released it then, pulled her hand back cautiously—it scuttled away from her, back under the cot.

"Let's give it another sardine. For a reward," Mo suggested.

When they left, she locked the door behind them. As they walked back, she told Mo about how Mrs. Cleaver had lost Mariners' Farm. "It's like an ancient curse," he commented. "Their nets shall be empty; their sons shall be driven from the land."

She clutched the key in her hand, looking around her at the soft green hills. A cow lowed from one, was answered from another. A rook crossed the sky alone.

After breakfast, he took off with his camera across the soggy fields. She built another fire and gathered her notebooks and sat down to write a poem. In the poem, a group of archaeologists came along to do a dig and found, among the disheveled bones and potsherds, a fading photograph of the whole tribe of those first ones, with their spears and babies, light-eyed longheads strapped into furs, lined up in their antique flesh and blood, staring at the earnest camera.

What do bones know? Nothing but themselves. What do eyes know? What they must forget. She got this far in five minutes, then spent the rest of the day fizzling out, trying to find a turning, a way to go.

In the afternoon, Mo came back and taped black paper over the bathroom window. He sealed all the cracks where light shined through the door. After supper, he set up the trays and developed the film he had taken during the day.

On Wednesday, Tom the postman brought the cat food out from the village, and she walked down to feed the gull by herself.

Mo spent the day painting. Late in the afternoon he packed his canvas stretcher, staple gun, some brushes and paints. He folded a couple of sweaters and shirts into the knapsack. When it was dark, he set up his equipment in the bathroom and printed the negatives. She sat on the rim of the tub and watched as he selected the first one, cut it from the strip, slipped it into the carrier. He closed the door and turned on the red light, took a sheet of paper out of the packet. He snapped on the light of the enlarger. She held the stopwatch and told him when it was time. He dropped the blank paper into the first tray. In the red light, the image began, loomed, and sharpened out of the fog until it was perfect. The stone barn in the bottom, the one that had made her cry. The chestnut tree cast its shadow down. He moved the print along the row of trays, fixing the image. "A present for you," he said, glancing sideways.

"Oh, Mo," she whispered. "I'm afraid we're really going to lose each other."

He put his arms around her. "No, we won't," he said. "We won't."

She went to bed at midnight.

She woke at two and he wasn't there.

She woke at four and he wasn't there.

He woke her at dawn. "I couldn't get myself to quit. I'll sleep on the train."

"I'll walk with you."

"On your feet then. Hustle."

In the bathroom a dozen prints were hung to dry. "Don't look at them now," he said. "It's late."

He carried the flight bag, full of his painting gear. She had the knapsack. The dawn wind lifted the smells of sea and dew and plowed earth around them. Not talking, covering the distance, they walked side by side on the track, with the same long, practical stride. A hare broke ahead of them, darted across the track, and leapt down onto the beach. It hopped away along the base of the rise with a noise against the pebbles like heavy human footsteps, running.

Finally, they climbed the road and turned into the village. The bus was already there. They ran down the street toward it. At the door of the bus, he took the knapsack off her back and looked at her attentively. "Don't worry, Gin," he said. "This is going to work out great."

He boarded the bus and put his things down. He reached into his pocket for the fare, turned, and ducked to wave happily at her. She stepped back, and through the bus window in front of her, Roger Simpson, on his way to work in Hudstone, inclined his head to her in serious greeting, the rough face, the long mobile lips, the stranded eyes. She leaned against the wall, feeling as though she were being lifted through the pane of dusty glass. Then he looked away. Mo took the seat in front of him, turned with his arm along the top of the seat to greet him. Roger Simpson nodded, said something, settled with his back to the window. Mo turned to her, wrote "Sunday" on the window, backward for her benefit, his narrow face drawn to a point of concentration. Then the bus moved out. She kissed her fingers to him; he waved once more.

On the way back, she stopped to feed and clean the gull.

At home, she put on the kettle and then went to look at the photographs hanging in the bathroom. The stone barn; the ridge with the profile of the fort from a thicket of thorn trees; Penzy Weaver in his shop among his looms and models of clipper ships; Mrs. Cleaver smiling beside her roses. The churchyard, Mariners' Chapel.

Their cottage from the track. Images of paradise. What paradise would boil down to, years from now.

She made her tea and toast and oatmeal and sat before the window, watching the birds. She spent the rest of the morning trying to bring the poem around. She changed the image—it was not a photograph of the tribal family that the archaeologists found. It was the photograph she had seen in *National Geographic,* of only the one man, naked, leaning over a promontory. But she couldn't take it where she wanted it to go. She was restless, fitful.

Finally, she closed her notebook and stalked out the back door, up through William Gullion's farm to the woods where the stone circle was supposed to be. But she couldn't find it. She had taken the map, but the Sheep Pen, as William Gullion had called it, wasn't noted on it, as far as she could tell. She looped through the woods, stopped looking for it, settled for just walking on the footpath under the great oaks.

She turned back down the slope toward evening and came out on the track, between the fisherman's hut and Matthew Cottage. Out in the mist on the bay were the two boats—when the men came home from their jobs in town, they often went out, if the weather and tides were right. She saw the dark figures at the oars. Roger Simpson was one of them, probably, but she couldn't tell which one. She stood watching for a while, then turned to go home. The sun was lost now in the western mist, as always. She walked back slowly, took an armload of wood from the stack, and went in to make a fire.

It was going to be the gull and the gray water and the fire and the poetry from here on. Winter would come soon; outside, distances would lengthen and shorten with the changes of light, but inside, the doors would close off one by one, the world would contract to the radius of the fire's warmth. She wanted to contract, too, to draw inward. But she felt herself turning out, instead, in spite of herself, turning unwillingly outward to where the boats now turned back toward shore, ran in against the pebbles.

She moved around the kitchen, fixing a salad, an omelette. She took her supper on a tray to eat before the fire. She turned the pages of her library book and drank her cider, and the wash of the waves was the only voice of the world.

Finally she laid the book down, put on her jacket, and went out again, feeling overtaken, flung out. She went to the same high place on the track. The boats were drawn up side by side on the beach, the cars and bicycles all gone. The moon, on the wane, had risen over the bay. It seemed to be dissolving into rather than shining through the haze that surrounded it, as though one side were disintegrating and flowing off as mist. A ship light, far out, came and went on the pulsing air. She turned back. The ridge, the track, the strip of beach, the luminous surf: a series of echoing curves. It was easy to imagine parallel lines curving out of infinity into darkness again. The squat shape of the cottage with its squares of light was the solitary interruption in that sweep.

Inside once more, she settled in her chair and watched the fire burn down, trying to draw back in from out there, out there. She fell asleep in the chair, woke at midnight, cold, for the fire had gone out.

○

Then it was Friday, and at five she was standing at the kitchen counter, holding a blue teacup, one knee propped on the wooden chair. She heard the bicycle tires whispering up the walk around the side of the cottage, and her blood went still and attentive as a dog on point. She put the cup down carefully in the saucer and waited, and heard the fall of the bicycle against the wall, and then his rap on the kitchen door.

"Hallo, Virginia."

"Hi. Come in." She stood aside, holding the door. Then they were facing each other in the vestibule beside the kitchen. "I was having some tea," she thought to say. "Would you like a cup?"

"No, thanks. I can't stop. I've got to get home." His graying hair curled wildly around his face. Another twenty years of it and he'd be a prophet, she thought—his hair would turn white, so would his eyes. They'd lead him in for soothsaying.

"Well, come into the other room, anyway—there's a little fire."

"All right."

She leaned against the fireplace with her arms at her sides. Her knees actually felt weak under her. *I willed him here, now what?* she thought. He chose to stand in the center of the room. He was wearing a checked wool jacket over the white coveralls. His loose, substantial body seemed almost clumsy in this room accustomed to lean people. "I talked to Mo," he began abruptly, as much as to say, *I have a reason for being here.* "On the bus the other morning. He mentioned that he'd have to be gone for a few days. I was wondering if you were managing to cope with the gull by yourself." He looked into her eyes as he spoke, as if by an effort of will. "I was at the hut so I thought I should just drop up here to check. I must say I'm surprised to see it's still hobblin' about." Now he allowed his eyes to glance off toward the fire.

"It comes to meet me now. I guess it knows which side its bread is buttered on." He smiled and nodded into the fire. "I can do it. I wear leather gloves. It doesn't seem as scared now as it did—it's got the mineral spirits connected with the food."

He nodded, seeming to be studying her mouth as she spoke. "Well, I'll be around part of the morning if you'd like some help tomorrow." Their eyes met, glanced off.

"Thank you."

He shifted his weight. He cocked his head and looked openly about the room. She looked too, saw it as he must—the colored notebooks strewn across the floor, the round table with the square Indian cloth thrown over, heaped with books, most of them open, haphazard bouquets in crocks and jars, candles melted down in wine bottles. Then he walked across the room to study the map of the county pinned to the wall under the stairs, his hands clasped behind his back like an admiral. "As a place on a map," he said, turning, with a quizzical, amused look, "we *are* rather promising."

She stared at him. "We must seem like children to you."

He looked back at her intently, the smile drifting away. "Yes, of course you do. How could you not? To me."

She turned to throw another log on the fire.

"Mo told me you'd be living for a while between here and London." It was a question.

She arranged the fire carefully with the poker, then said without turning, "What he means is that by and large he'll be living in London and I'll be living here."

"Oh." The word was like a breath expelled and in the silence that followed she couldn't breathe, hearing the flat spoken-out truth of her words, taking in her situation for the first time, feeling the air shift, realign itself.

"He likes it here," she explained, finally, on Mo's behalf, "but he doesn't know how to use this world. It doesn't work with his painting." She replaced the poker and turned to glance at him. She shrugged and smiled.

He came across the room, stopped beside her at the mantel. "You've collected some fossils."

"I find some." They stood before the fire, their arms almost grazing. Close enough for her to smell the salt trapped in the fibers of his sweater. If she wanted to address him, she would have to turn her head and tilt it up.

He picked up the gold stone, turned it over in his hand, looked at it distractedly. "A sea urchin," he said, finally, as though to himself. He put it down without looking at her, shoved his hands into his pockets. There didn't seem to be anything else to say. So he said, "Well, I'll be off." But neither of them moved. They stood side by side, staring at the fire. "Children in the best possible sense, I mean," he said finally, abruptly.

She moved away from the mantel then to switch on the lamp beside the chair. "You mean playing nicely."

"Well, playing seriously."

"But playing."

"Yes, I suppose so."

"Do you disapprove?"

"Of course not—who am I to disapprove? Or approve, for that matter. I just watch. From where I am."

She stayed beside the lamp, not wanting to look up; she didn't think she could bear to look at him now, with this distinction between them stated so. At his face, like the hills in this crescent, tamed down, smoothed over, as though the flood had passed over *it*, too, worn it down: *from where I am.* Still, she spoke from the heart when she said, "I don't think you're a fool to stay here." The words flew out to him. She would like to have told him how deeply this place had lodged in her, to tell him what she had seen from the hill fort.

But he met her cautiously, skeptically, and again she felt like a child. "No?"

"I'd do the same if I were you."

He nodded, as though to acknowledge her kindness. "But you're not," he said then, and these words did not fly. They seemed meant to stop flight. They brought her head up.

"No," she felt obliged to agree, blushing, feeling reprimanded for her presumption. "I'm not."

"If I were *you*—"

"Don't say," she said, laughing, holding up her hand.

"I can't imagine anyway," he said, also laughing, as though he'd almost caught himself by surprise. "I wouldn't know how to begin to imagine your choices." And then he pulled himself up. "*Well,*" he said, and they moved together toward the kitchen.

"Thank you for checking," she said. "Maybe I'll see you tomorrow morning then."

"Right."

"I may need help with the wings—I've been worried about how to manage them." She went before him to the door, held it open. "Good night."

As he passed her, her body felt like something under the sea, like seaweed bending all one way.

And then there was nothing to do but to lie still, wait, will nothing more, leave it up to him, wait till morning.

○

The door of the hut was not locked. She opened it and he was waiting there, leaning by the window. She closed the door. The gull came bustling around her feet.

"I haven't fed it," he said. "I thought it would be best if only you fed it."

She opened the tin. She stooped to set it down before the gull. It jabbed into it; over every morsel it shook its head, arced its wings. "He's feeling better," she said.

"We'll have a job getting rid of this fellow—he'll go right out and get himself mucked up again, to get the grub."

She rose, brushing her hands together, lifted her eyes to his face.

"I can't stop thinking of you," he said in a low, perplexed voice, as though describing a mysterious malady.

"Oh," she breathed.

He looked at a loss, he looked as though he were suffering. *Nor I of you,* she wanted to say, but couldn't. Instead, she reached her hand out to him, and they came blindly together then. Her face was against the harsh wool of his sweater. She rubbed her cheek back and forth against it, hard. He lifted and turned her face. "Don't. Don't." For a moment his hands came to rest warmly against her neck, under her hair; then they fell away. His body shifted out of her hands. "Oh my dear," he said. "There's no hope for this." His face was above her, weary, calm. "You know, don't you."

"Yes." Her arms fell by her sides, her head fell heavily sideways. "I wasn't thinking of hope. I was thinking of nothing. Of you."

He raised her face. "I'm here, you see. All my life is here. I've chosen. I'm not free, as you are." His eyes were like left-behind pools in his seaworn face. She let her gaze fall to his shoulders. He was the man who had pulled in the nets when they were heavy with fish. But he was not for her. Not even for now. Never. For he was not free, as she was.

She stepped away from him, turned to look at the gull, still knicking and nabbing at the tin of cat food with its blood-spotted beak. Then she went to stand at the window, looking out over the still water and the golden margin. "You'll have to deal with the gull," she said finally. "He's yours, anyway. I just happened to find him. I'm sorry. I know it will be a bother."

"You're going to London?" he asked, from his distance.

She considered that possibility. She imagined herself walking, her hand on Mo's arm, along a street of Georgian houses. He was pointing things out to her. She felt sharply the pleasure of it, the delight that passed between them as they moved together along this perfect street. And then she gave it up. She turned away from London, and away from Mo. "No. It would just be another place I'd have to leave. This is the last place I'm planning to leave."

"Back to America, then."

She turned from the window. "When you say it, it sounds like the New World." They smiled at one another affectionately, as though they'd been friends a long time.

"I suppose that's what it still is, to me. I'm a bit behind the times."

"Well, new or not, that's where I'm going. Back to America." She fished the iron key out of her pocket. She crossed the room and put it down on the table beside him, keeping her hand on it. "But if I were you, if I were you"—his name was in her heart, but she couldn't utter it—"I'd never give this place up, not in a million years."

He reached out and touched her face with gentle curiosity, one cheek, then the other. "Oh, I'll stay," he said, in his straight voice, smiling at her. "Whatever the future is, I'll deal with it here, as best I can."

"I wish, though. . . ." She stopped herself, then said it anyway. "In some other life, you might have come with me. We might have just run away."

He clasped one of her hands in both of his, turning her silver ring with his thumb, looking up from it, smiling deeply into her eyes. "Yes. And who would have taken care of the gull?"

She rose quickly to kiss his cheek.

Then she went through the door.

Later in the morning, she caught a ride into the village with Tom. From there she caught the bus over the hills to Hudstone, where she rented a car, charging it with her credit card. She drove back to the village, put a check for the November rent in Mrs. Cleaver's mailbox, along with a note. Then she drove down along the track to the cottage.

She packed her suitcases and her books and loaded them in the car. She made the bed, emptied the small refrigerator, washed the dishes and the kitchen floor, threw out the dead flowers. It was so simple; that was all there was to do. She wrote a letter to Mo, left it on the round table. He'd be back the next afternoon. She weighted it with the sea urchin fossil.

At the very last minute, she gathered up the photographs Mo had printed and slipped them into her shoulder bag. *They aren't yours. And anyway, you don't need them,* she told herself sternly. *You've seen enough; you'll remember.* But she wanted them, she wanted them, she couldn't bear to leave them.

She put on her parka and closed the door behind her. She turned the key in the ignition, backed down the drive, and headed along the track toward the village. On the ridge above her, the sun had defined the rough indentations of the old fort. She passed the fisherman's hut. The door was bolted; the two boats were hoisted underneath the tin roof of the shed. Then she turned on the road away from the water and drove up the hill to the village. Penzy Weaver was walking up the street from his shop to the pub for lunch. He raised his hand in puzzled greeting as she waved. Past Mrs. Cleaver's house, past the church, the manor house she drove. She didn't look back. If she had, she knew what she would have seen—the golden chapel on Aldercombe Hill, facing the sea for six centuries. Let it be safe six centuries more, she prayed. Though no light will shine from its tower again, to guide ships through this dying sea. Let it stand somehow, anyhow.

But she didn't look back; it was all turning to photographs now. She'd seen enough. She'd seen what she had been obliged to see. And what she'd wanted to see. She turned north now, up the ridge, and then over it, on the way to Black Grange, to London, to Heathrow, and then to America, her own random country, the New World.

The Author

Mary Ann Taylor-Hall's short fiction has appeared in *The Sewanee Review, The Colorado Quarterly, The Kenyon Review, The Paris Review, The Florida Review, Ploughshares, The Chattahoochee Review,* and *Shenandoah,* . Her work has won a PEN/Syndicated Fiction Award and has been anthologized in *Best American Short Stories.* She has received grants from the National Endowment for the Arts and the Kentucky Arts Council. Her first novel, *Come and Go, Molly Snow,* was published in 1995. Taylor-Hall lives on a farm on the county line between Harrison and Scott counties, in Kentucky, with her husband James Baker Hall.

James Baker Hall

Colophon

Set in Zapf Calligraphic.
Designed by Charles Casey
Martin. Printed and bound
by Thomson-Shore.

NEW HANOVER COUNTY PUBLIC LIB.
3 4200 00546 2276